THE
ESSENTIALS

A Manifesto

DAVID TROMBLAY

Whisk(e)y Tit
VT & NYC

Published in the United States by Whisk(e)y Tit: www.whiskeytit.com. If you wish to use or reproduce all or part of this book for any means, please let the author and publisher know. You're pretty much required to, legally.

ISBN 978-1-952600-06-7

Library of Congress Control Number: 2020951370

First Whisk(e)y Tit paperback edition.

"I never grow tired of the sound of coyotes."

—Craig Clevenger, 8:14 PM 11/15/
2020 PST

THE LADY IN THE
BASEMENT

I found a notice in my mailbox at the warehouse telling me to report here, I think. I've never been down here before.

Oh?

I'm a courier.

I see.

Who do I see to get the vaccinated?

No, no, no. Not here.

Oh, I'm sorry to have disturbed you.

No, it's no bother. You're in the right place. Name?

Jon. Jonathan Shaddox.

Mr. Shaddox, can you please close my door?

Yes. yes, of course.

Sit sit sit. Can I see your badges? And your license.

Yessum. I have the notice right here as well.

Oh, there's no need. I don't need to see it. Please recycle it once we're done here today.

Okay.

What's this?

Sorry, that's my disabled veterans ID. No good now. Not anymore. Here's my license.

You're disabled?

Yes, but more like put out to stud. Got old.

Oh. Were you in the desert wars?

Early on. First fifteen years.

My nephew was sent over, too. What did you do over there that got you put out to stud, as you say?

Am I getting the vaccine today, or relieved?

You haven't got your shot in several years, Mr. Shaddox. Is that right?

They focus on the care of the older guys at the veteran's hospital, mostly.

And?

And I was told they only get the serum meant for those of advancing years. Those with already failing immunity.

I see.

I mean, I could get that shot, but I'd have to take time off to do so, and, again, I was told the serum they'd inoculate me with would most likely be a waste with me being so young. I don't understand how it all works, that's just what they've told me when I asked.

Who told you this?

A woman I've known since grade school runs the

lab and the immunizations clinic over there. She's always told me not to bother.

And you thought it would be less risky to walk around without it?

Each day off from work is $100 off my paycheck.

I see.

How are you here now and not working?

I wasn't asked to come, I got a summons, I say, and wave the printed notice I pulled from my mailbox earlier that AM..

I see. And you can't afford the time off work.

No, ma'am. I was put out to stud. That's not as metaphorical as you might think.

So, you have children to pay for?

Yessum.

But you haven't taken any sick days?

Ma'am?

Ever.

No, just earned vacation days.

So I see.

How long have you worked as a medical courier?

A few years now.

Looks like five.

That many?

Yes. And you've never gotten a shot.

Nope.

That wasn't a question, Mr. Shaddox, I have your files on my screen.

You have that information?

I do, you should get a plaque. You've never taken a single sick day.

I've never really paid much attention. I guess I've never taken ill, ma'am. Never enough so to willingly lose out on the remittance. Though, that is how I was raised: don't see the doctor unless you're dying. And, while I served, too, going to sick call was a sure-fire way to stifle your career. So, it kind of became instinct to stay away.

Interesting. You've never taken ill—in five years' time? Is that right?

I've had a sore throat here and there. The sniffles a time or two, but it never lasts more than a few hours. Never enough to bother me. I'm in and out of the weather all day, so that's it mostly. Pollen in the springtime and summer, I suppose.

I see. That's understandable. Don't get me wrong, you're not being reprimanded for keeping healthy. That's not it. That's not why you were called here today, Mr. Shaddox.

I know it's policy now that I'm with you guys. I'll get it. The shot, that is.

No, there's no need.

I'm f—

Excuse me?

Am I being relieved of my appointment, fired?

Mr. Shaddox, you've worked as a medical courier for five years now. There are four clinics on your route, correct? And you visit those laboratories how many times a day?

Five. I take five laps around the city each day. Ten-hour workday. It's just shy of two hours for each lap. Lunches at red lights, I laugh. Wish I was making that last part up, I tell her.

The amount of time you have spent around the afflicted, the infected, the infested people of this city, Mr. Shaddox — is staggering. You understand that?

You're not a fan of the ailing people who frequent your facilities, ma'am?

That's not what I'm driving at here.

Is this a reprimand? Umm, Ma'am.

It's a new employee evaluation, in a roundabout way, Mr. Shaddox. Nothing more.

We're acquiring carriers. Bringing you into our fold, our family, so to speak, Mr. Shaddox. You'll get a new access badge, one that expands where you'll be allowed unescorted.

Expand? Are you adding more stops to my route?

In time we most certainly will, while others will be eliminated entirely. But for now, the new badge will identify you as ours rather than an outside hire. That should allow you to work more smoothly, more efficiently, without slowing you down waiting for one of ours to sign off and verify that you've done what we pay you to do.

I like the sound of that.

It should also stop people from asking who you

are and what you are doing when they see you wander into their workspace.

That'll speed things along too.

People get curious when they see a new face.

Well, yes, they're protective when it comes to their patient's privacy and whatnot. I'd expect them to be. I don't get bent out of shape when it happens.

Donors.

Excuse me?

Donors, Mr. Shaddox. Donor is the preferred terminology. Think of those who visit the laboratories as donors. Just people donating a specimen.

Yessum.

Now that you're one of ours, you'll be self-contained, so to speak. There'll be no need for a chain of custody with the things you carry. You can simply carry them. You'll still have to scan them, and we will be able to see where it is they are at any given time—as long as they are with you. Understand?

Yes, I won't have to repeat any steps because of the two systems not being able to talk to one another any longer.

That's exactly it. Exactly right.

Now, we'll need you to fill out forms with your current information, so we may update our database. We need to make sure you get paid, Mr.

Shaddox. You're married to one of our doctors, is that right?

That's right.

And the CV our HR department has from your former employer says you're a doctor, of the academic variety. Yet, you're doing this to pay the bills?

It allows me time to muse and write. And you get a driver who understands the application and importance of military precision.

You don't need to fill out those forms. I'll merge your file with that of your wife's.

That's appreciated. Thank you.

You are welcome. Now, I should mention we're in an interim period here, but we are looking at you as the potential lead carrier for this district, Mr. Shaddox.

Courier?

Carrier. We have our own verbiage here.

Understood.

Occupational health will want to see you for a physical, blood work, and so on.

Okay.

You should do that today, you'll be credited for a full day's work.

Thank you.

Someone such as yourself is quite the find for us, Mr. Shaddox, what with us losing so many personnel to excessive and—if I may be frank—questionable sick days. But you're the antithesis, aren't you? She says with a smile. It's no wonder you were put out to stud. Your children must have never missed a day of school.

They take after their mother in that aspect, I'm afraid. They're little germ factories. Always getting their mother sick with something new.

But not you?

Knock on wood.

Well, with that being the case, we just might have to order up some additional blood work on you, Mr. Shaddox. There are some people here who'll be curious to see what makes someone such as yourself tick. This is a teaching hospital, after all. Virology finds the immune fascinating—from what I've heard discussed, at least.

The immune?

People like you, Mr. Shaddox, outwardly impervious to illness.

I get all my medical care from the veterans' hospital, ma'am. That's where my doctor is. How much is my care through the hospital as an employee? Or—is it possible for me to deny coverage and stick with them? I need my check to be fat as can be, see? That's why I ask.

No, your care is cost-free. Completely on us. We want you to continue to be healthy here. We might even be able to learn a thing or two from you, Mr. Shaddox. Help the people of this district. And we share information with our other locations, of course. Never names, just medical findings.

Of course, I expected as much.

How's that?

The medical journals the mail room sometimes sends out to the satellite clinics.

Oh, you mean the distribution center.

Understood.

Departments are being given new roles, new names. It's the Memorandum and Correspondence Distribution Center, but that's a mouthful.

They don't wear scrubs anymore, I noticed.

No, they do not.

They don't wear business casual or business professional either. You can hardly tell they work here, yet alone have jobs.

That's the idea, Mr. Shaddox. They may wear whatever. You know who they are because you see them in their workspace, but we'd prefer if they were to blend in with visitors. They control the company's correspondences, we'd like them to go unnoticed, be unidentifiable, understand?

Yessum.

Great. Occupational health is expecting you now. So are they in the lab.

REMARKS BY DELEGATE BURR TO THE UNITED NATIONS GENERAL ASSEMBLY

United Nations Headquarters
New York, New York
June 14, 2030
09:02 A.M. EDT

DELEGATE BURR: Mr. President, Mr. Secretary General, fellow delegates, ladies, and gentlemen: Seventy-five years after the founding of the United Nations, it is worth reflecting on what, together, the members of this body have helped to achieve. However, it too is time to give equal credence to our failures. The latter is why I have chosen to speak at this summit today—to be the voice of reason to rise above the rest and usher in a new era in global policy, rather than allow the rhetorical mutterings of do-gooders to yammer on any longer and bring about any more stagnation. Our successes have led to this excess.

Let me begin by addressing the current conversation that has led us to this global imbalance, this catastrophe of which there is no longer an escape. Sustainable and renewable resources such as locally sourced and organic food, zero emission power plants and transportation, as well as access to medical care and clean drinking water for every single, solitary person on the planet, regardless of position, is nothing more than a deranged fairy tale. We are too many for this host to handle. There is no happy ending here, ladies, and gentlemen. If one does exist, it certainly is not one which we have sold to the trusting people of this world for far too long. We achieved what we set out to without considering the consequences of it becoming an actuality, rather than a long-echoed bicameral campaign promise. Achieving this utopism has placed a

Band-Aid over a festering issue: our cities have simply swelled too large, enveloping what was once our forests and farmland once reserved for the yielding of commodities and the grazing of livestock. This bloating of our cities has led to the perforating of our borders, if I may address the elephant in the room while I have the podium. Now, yes, most of our cities have managed to produce food on rooftops and outcropped balconies. And if we can allow ourselves to stop pretending this measure is anything more than an aesthetic trend which only feeds the minuscule numbers of those who live within these suburban skyscrapers, especially now that we've met and exceeded our planet's maximum occupancy—and only in those places capable of sustained mild climates. The rest of the globe, which suffers daily from unpredictable extremes, will starve if these measures become their only means of sustenance. Especially considering how I hear the daily birth rate is reaching double that of the rate of death. Our successes have led to this excess.

The soil of our farmlands across the Great Plains will not maintain its fertility much longer. Every day we inch closer to another occurrence of the dust bowl of the nineteen-thirties. Atop this issue, I've read the weakened topsoil is no longer able to filter and cleanse our groundwater. For this reason, we are proposing to relinquish the protected status of our national prairielands and parklands, so they may be better utilized; the land there has never been farmed and therefore never overfarmed. We know without action many will die of thirst and malnutrition in the coming years. Many more will die from drinking the only water available, water which we cannot make safe for them. While this figure may seem crude, we can only support fifteen percent of the world's current population. Your outliers who live in the townships, and villages, and rural annexations must be brought into your cities for their protection unless you are content with your people suffering a protracted extermination. Our successes have led to this excess.

With our swelled cities enveloping our former forest and farmlands, there is simply not enough mature leafy vegetation remaining to produce enough oxygen in a season with our now overly robust populace. I am told asthma will become more grave a diagnosis than cancer was to our grandparents' generation. One tree can produce enough fresh oxygen for ten people to breathe. But I challenge you, when you return home, walk your cities' streets and count the trees. Ours are so cramped and choked from sunlight at the street level that not even moss will flourish any longer. What we lacked the foresight to realize is how the forests we leveled to make room for fields of solar panels and turbines once acted like enormous filters, filters that cleansed the air we exhaled. STEM will not be able to fix this.

How do we do this? How do we rid the world of this issue of overpopulation?

Just as we commissioned Buffalo Bill Cody to control the bloated bison herds and in turn make the Savages dependent on food of our choosing, we must now suspend all social programs; successful as they may have proven; as many generations as it may take to perfect and implement. Our successes have led to this excess.

Every nation on every continent must follow suit for our actions to be anything but a drop in the bucket. Every citizen, who pays their own way and takes care of their own children, must subsidize the 109,631,000 others no more. Each state, county, city, municipality, must become introspective and find their biggest drains. They alone will fix this imbalance. They will have no blueprint. They will ensure their community's own survival or lack thereof. They will decide what will be repealed. They will no longer allow indebtedness to flourish. Humanity must be strong. We, as their leaders, must be strong. (Applause)

We, too, must immediately cease

providing aid and mediation to all warring and developing countries not represented here today. They must no longer be recognized. The problem of their civil unrest and societal imbalances will have to seek settlement from within. Travel, to and from these countries, must cease as well. Though, the newest medical treatments and pharmaceuticals should continue to be gifted to these nations. They must not revolt. We do not need their insurgencies spilling into our borders. They must be convinced all that can be done has been done, and, at that, they will become convinced to seek sanctuary from within.

Visas should be immediately revoked or suspended, and all renewals froze. Refugees need not be set to their homelands. We need not eat up any more of our already precious resources. Isolationism will be key to bringing about balance. People must stay where they are. We need only the obedient for this cause—the dogs of this new war—not the fleas on the dogs back. This will be the truest test of patriotism our nations have ever endured. (Applause)

We seek a new breed of patriot. It has been a decade since we have disarmed the citizens of the world. I have been assured every veteran of every war of the past hundred years has died or become invalid. Still, we have listed each of ours as potential domestic terrorists. Those remaining must not be allowed to travel or congregate. The time for us to implement these actions is now.

(Applause)

The media has been removed from this chamber and must be denied access to all heads of state, assemblies of Congress, parliaments, and senates heretofore if we are to succeed in this endeavor. The Center for Disease Control, the World Health Organization, International Federation of Red Cross and Red Crescent Societies must all be kept in the dark. UNICEF was dismantled earlier today on my order. Doctors Without Borders will no longer be able to receive funding of any sort nor will the Peace Corps. Oxfam and Amnesty International will share in their fate as well. On my recommendation, Marshall law is being implemented, quietly, to usher in these changes. All peacekeepers must be called back inside their perspective borders. We will abandon all foreign-based installations. The land and resources therein will be handed over to the host countries. BRAC has already begun this process, as some of you may be aware. This will make some of you vulnerable. We, as a species, can no longer protect the weak. We have done this with the animals, locking them away in zoos and aquariums in order to give them a second chance rather than letting them die off and make room for the next evolutionary achievement. We too have created something of a zoo of our populace, protecting every citizen, ensuring no harm can come to them, leaving us all weakened, vulnerable. No more. (Applause)

I regret to inform you global

banking and international trade will no doubt suffer through this. Capitalism will fall. Currency and exchange rates will not see us through this, only a means of basic and fair bartering will manage to see us through. Import and export will go through a greater evolution than any organism that has called this planet of ours home. Desert nations only need offer oil and petroleum products. Those nations who can still produce cotton and wheat and corn and fruits and other vegetables, together with the nations who can still produce livestock, will come to embrace a symbiosis never seen before at any time in human history—for it is the only way we can assure that the future will be brighter for my children, and for yours.

Thank you very much. (Applause)

END

09:58 A.M. EDT

SAME OLD, SAME OLD

You here to pick me up? Name's Bartlo Bogdan. That's with a b not a d.

Nope. You are not in my scanner. Please close the door.

You sure? You're not the one they sent to pick me up?

Not unless you're pumped full of formaldehyde, packed in ice, on your way to see some medical students for show and tell.

Not yet I ain't. Didn't mean to bother you.

Okay, that's nice. Close the door now—if you would be so kind, I say and sneak my hand down between the seats.

Why is it so heavy, or am I so old all a sudden?

All the way! I say at the top of my lungs after not hearing the door latch shut and swing open again.

Do you go by the name Shaddox? Another voice asks and takes a seat next to me.

I recoil away from the navigation screen with the tire iron in hand.

You're the Carrier, yeah? You're the one who's supposed to show me around. I'm a Runner. Or will be, if I can cut it. I guess that's how it works, right? he says, leaving the question to flutter about the cab between the two of us before offering another: Or are you going to bash my skull in with that tire iron you got in your grip there?

The door clicks shut.

Right, that's how it works. If, I say, and set the tire iron back down between the seats.

There's somebody walking up.

Him? Yeah. He doesn't seem to like me much.

Why not?

Don't know. Never asked. He talks in tongues, far as I can tell.

Tongues?

Gibberish. It's nonsensical, and doesn't resemble English the least little bit.

What's he doing with that walking stick.

Walking.

It's as tall as him.

Yup, sure is.

What's all over the top?

Ahh...to him? Trophies, talismans, trinkets, stuff he's pulled off other people or out of the trash—you name it. That's my best guess anyway. Feel free to hop on out and ask him, I laugh.

Unamused he regards all that adorns the man's staff and says, Looks like festival beads and a bit of chain with a blade attached. And that there looks like somebody's ponytail.

Scalp too, I nod. That ponytail is still attached to the scalp if you look a little closer. It caught my attention a good while back. It's real all right. He salted it some, but it still looks a little more weathered every time I come across him. And those aren't festival beads. Not from any sort of party you'd want to attend, at least. He probably pulled them from the ass of a corpse thinking he'd found a tracking node. Now he's displaying them for all the world to see. So they'll know he knows what's happening. Or maybe he's hoping they will come for him.

Scalp? Like as in scalp scalp? he says and traces his own hairline with a finger.

Peeled off like the leather from a baseball.

How do you know all this if you've never spoken to him?

I've lived long enough to know what I'm looking at when I see a thing. That, and when you see someone as much as he and I see one another you just kind of fill in the blanks for each other. Have to entertain yourself somehow, you know? People are fascinating, even the boring ones, especially the boring ones.

How's he boring?

There's no secrecy with him. He lives out in the wild. He never goes behind closed doors.

He's not going to let us leave.

Well, that's his mission, see? He thinks himself a crusader of sorts. Thinks I'm evil. Or this building is, I say and push the ignition, sparking the engine to life. Once it warms, I hit the lever and bring the hydraulics to life which raises and flexes the v-plow in a silent word of warning. You ever drove before?

He rocks his head to the right and left telling me he hasn't.

Look here, down is up, up is down, left moves the blades right, right moves them to the left. When you kill the engine, the blades will settle to the ground on their own time. But with the engine running like it is right now, you can drop them down fast enough to take off his toes. You got it?

Yes.

You look scared.

Unsure.

Nah, scared is good. Stick with scared. Scared will keep you cautious, keep you alive out here. Get it?

You, you're smiling at all this.

Like a dog wagging his tail—

Wagging its—

Right before it bites you. I am the calm in this shitstorm. Have to be. It's what they ask of me. This is what I call a Tuesday morning. Did you buckle in all the way?

Think so.

Good, I say, and slide the lever to angle the

blades toward the passenger side. Once the gauge tells me the brakes have let out I lunge the vehicle forward fast as it'll go, making the vagabond pirouette away from my wheels and swan dive down into the dirt where he covers his ears to block out the reverberations of the engine coming off the surrounding concrete loud enough to loosen what few teeth there are left in his head. The blades break through the infrared and the door lifts letting us out into the awaiting district of Duluth.

Is he going to get up okay?

I shake my head left to right, shrug, sing, *Ain't nobody gonna slow me down, oh no, I got to keep on moving,* and flash my eyebrows up my forehead as high as they'll go.

SCAVENGING OF THE SUB-URBAN FRINGES CONTINUES

By Gregory Nesmith
February 4, 2039

DULUTH — The resettlement of the North American districts may be long-remembered as a devastating blow to our once-cherished way of life, but the scavenging of the former residential zones by the nonessential citizens is without a doubt more menacing of a nightmare. The unforecastable and unseasonable meteorological extremes which have become a daily reality inflict immense and irreversible damage on our ecosystem as well as the households where we once laid our heads to rest at night. But when the nonessentials adopted savagery as a way of life, they then purposely shat on the final vestige of our once great first-world civilization. Therefore, President Burr signed a preemptive Executive Order today which will strike down any claim they may attempt to make concerning the doctrine of adverse possession. In short, they will not be permitted as much as squatter's rights that could have otherwise made life as a community possible for them.

Reports of their depravity trickled in before the first of the essentials could be loaded onto buses and driven to the towers erected in the circumcenter of the district. A sub-urban market atop Duluth's Miller Hill was one of the first stores targeted; its inventory of fishing and shooting supplies was first to vanish. Shortly thereafter, dozens of scavengers emptied clothing department stores, jewelers, and liquor stores, in full view of broadcast television drones deployed to monitor the events as they unfold. Even State Militiamen have reportedly abandoned their orders to enforce martial law and instead scavenged alongside the others, hauling cases of beer and alcohol through waist-deep snow, while other members of the unit are said to have used trash cans to haul away clothing, shoes, and truckloads of electronics. In a video clip obtained by the Public Broadcasting Service, men and women — who are believed to be policing agents — were seen stripping a shopping mall bare in the nearby town of Herman.

Another scavenger stole a frontend loader belonging to a roadway maintenance crew and drove it better than a kilometer in order to break a steel security gate away from the concrete façade of a shuttered pharmacy, allowing a countless number to pour into the building and eviscerate the stocks of medicines and medical supplies. The fear here is the question of their intent with these medicines they now possess and what concoctions can be created with the unlimited combinations of the different medicines — or worse — whether they intend to somehow introduce their creations to the populace brought to live within the towers. The dollar amount of the lost pharmaceuticals is inestimable, according to a hospital press release. Some were seen fleeing the pharmacy with armfuls of diapers and baby formula. Others were clutching single bottles of pills in each hand while they sprinted in the direction of what is believed to be an encampment some of the scavengers have established in the spiderwebbed network of abandoned dormitories at the former state university. The Duluth district council also warns how some individuals may be gathering bombmaking materials for which they could unleash untold acts of violence on the residents of the towers. They continued with their word of warning that under no circumstances should anyone attempt to return to their former household for any reason. This same public address stated how scavengers entered the parking garage of an unnamed affluent high-rise to strip cars of their batteries and homes of their smoke alarms. Scavengers also stole a specially-adapted bus from a hospice facility. They too relieved a truck filled with food belonging to the policing agency of all it had to offer. Unfortunately, the collapse of civility did not end with the scavenging of property. This mob of scavengers is also reported to have attacked essentials. One cannot help but wonder whether they hope to become active in the organ trade.

Duluth District Council Chief Doyle Byrnes described the reports brought to him concerning the savagery of the scavengers: "Rapes are happening at alarming rates — and men — sodomized; there are individuals who are being beaten until unresponsive. And because of the remoteness of the sub-urban fringes, they are assuredly being left for dead." He sent 200 policing agents to quell the unrest, but they were overwhelmed by a mob of scavengers displaying what could be best described as training and tactics stereotypical of those used by the North American Armed Forces while executing high-value target raids during the desert wars. Policing agents trained as designated marksmen have been ordered to take up various positions along the rooftops of the towers and the neighboring hospital in order to reach and repel any encroaching scavengers. The policing agency would prefer not to have to perpetually patrol the district with roving agents. Essential citizens should be allowed to move about freely and without the constant presence of policing and surveillance agents looming about. "Not all the corpses turning up in Duluth are exposure victims. Some have been shot to death, others lynched," Chief Byrnes said. The National District Resettlement and Closure Agency is almost sure to soon be forced to operate, director Emogene Swan said, "beyond conditions requiring the enactment of Martial Law. Instead, essential citizens will see their former neighborhoods become a battlefield embroiled in urban warfare if these conditions continue."

Chief Byrnes reminded the other council members how, "There were those who proposed early on for the on-sight shooting of the nonessentials who were found scavenging the homes and businesses of the essential citizens once they were moved into the towers. We should have listened. Nipped this in the bud. The drones can do more than look onhelplessly. We should have listened, ladies and gentlemen. And not for the reason that I believe the property of the essentials is more valuable than the life of the nonessentials — as some might try to claim— but because I believe that if history has taught us one thing, it is when property is no longer protected from those who scavenge, then neither is human life. Once the nonessentials figure out how to get away with scavenging — which they already have — then they surely will, given enough time — realize they can do whatever they please. And don't kid yourself here, we — this entire council — are all culpable for our inaction."

As with any panel or council propped up to preside over a people, there are those in its midst who believe it is right and just to look for reasons behind the unreasonable actions of strangers.

"Imagine if the people of New York City were abandoned this way in the days following 9/11. Who here cares to entertain the thoughts concerning what they would have done had they been in such a situation as the nonessential citizens of the Duluth district following the resettlement of the essential citizens?" said Thos Cangelosi, Vice Chief of the Duluth District Council. "Once there is no food being shipped to the grocery stores, no more fresh water moving through the district plumbing — or sanitation — who here can honestly speculate what that unprecedented level of desperation could cause one to do — especially, once it happens to a mob? The nonessentials are attempting to provide for their children and aging family members alike."

The argument was quickly silenced by Council Chief Byrnes who told Cangelosi if he believes "these were the nonessential's sentiments when they began pillaging jewelry counters and thieving pallets of alcohol along with the raping they've committed, then Cangelosi, by all means, feel free to join them in the sub-urban fringes." Chief Byrnes also added that if Vice Chief Cangelosi felt so strongly, then perhaps he "may in fact have a moral obligation to join the nonessentials as well." Cangelosi offered no rebuttal.

When the Duluth district plunged into disorder, The National Press cautioned readers away from jumping to any black and white moral judgments. "Scavenging," Ida Harris wrote on the homepage of the National Tribune, "is far more complex than the thousand words a picture can articulate." And how the myriad of stills and videos of scavengers scurrying off with electronics and alcohol is somehow inarticulate, he did not clarify. Though, he did lean on a quote from another likeminded individual who offered their insight to help those — such as myself — to understand the so-called "nuances of scavenging." Justice Studies Professor Victoria Haschemeyer of the Superior University said, "What might appear from the outsider's vantage point will undoubtedly look like thievery. Especially, to those essential citizens who were forced to abandon a vast majority of their personal property — rather than the simple act of those deemed to be nonessential citizens hoarding goods which can one day be bartered or brought to pawnbrokers, so they can buy or acquire that which they need for their family's survival."

Most citizens have little issue identifying the dichotomy separating desperation and the shameless acts of the scavengers, which have now inarguably spiraled downward to the same sort of scourge the merciless savages once forced the forefathers of this great land to endure. This truth is no different than that of how conservatism and nationalism are never more needed than during the days when we — the huddled masses — must sacrifice for this great land of ours. Indeed, far too many people acted animalistically during the resettlement of the towers, yet, an immeasurable number of conglomerations and corporate philanthropists answered those actions with charity and warmth in the hope to make lifefor those inside the towers one of inconceivable luxury.

When voicing his concern for the survival of the English language in his lauded "Lanterns and Lances," James Thurber wrote: "There are two kinds of light — the glow that illumines, and the glare that obscures." Each of us chooses where on the spectrum we belong. In the district of Duluth, the essentials and the nonessentials have made their decision seen by the entire nation.

NATAL DAY

They knew the day would come, don't kid yourself.

They planned for it?

That's their job. They're planners. They made preparations.

Wait. Who are...they?

What? They? No one you know. Everyone else is they. Stick with that understanding and you'll do just fine out here.

So, you're saying they did this?

Yes, protocols were put in place for the eventuality.

What eventuality? You're a—conversing with you is a bit like pulling teeth.

The birth of the ten-billionth citizen. *Citizen* as the people have come to call her.

Yes, I know the tale of Citizen. She died a long time ago.

No, no. No, she didn't. She didn't live long. That's the part of the story that's changed. That's just what people have come to conclude, for whatever reason. But she did live. That—that part is still true. People like to think her story took place a long time ago and pretend that things have always been the way they are now. But it just is not so.

No one ever told me when she lived, just that she did live.

Oh, I assure you she did. Her name, however, I couldn't tell you. I'll tell you something else about her: when she is spoken of by those who were alive the day she was born, her name is spoken of with the same mix of emotions as *Ground Zero*.

Like *Patient Zero* from the preparation manuals?

No, they're not the same thing. Those are guides for worst-case scenarios. Although, it could be argued the sentiment is the same. You've read them? — the preparation manuals.

I've memorized them.

Parroting something and knowing something is altogether different.

Were you born before she was?

I worked that day. She is our citizen, you know?

Our citizen?

Yes, our citizen. Born in our birthing unit. Weighed, measured, cleansed, cataloged, all by the Benedictine Sisters. I remember it as distinctly as anything.

Is that so?

Absolutely. It was the day the public-address amplifiers were switched off.

PA amplifiers? The hospital halls are silent. They must be—to maintain the solemn tranquility for the infirm as they transition.

Yes, now.

When did they allow music?

Incessantly. Brahms' Cradle Song interrupted muzak to announce each new birth.

Muzak?

Songs without anyone singing to the melody, like karaoke sans the slurred screeches of an inebriated balladeer.

And it was switched off for her birth?

Mmm— No, it was switched off because of her birth.

So, yes and no? The correlation is still there, though?

Well, it wasn't my hand that turned the dial. But it is said the Sister who kept the hallways filled with song knew what was to come, so she switched off the speakers and left. Couldn't bear it. A silent prayer to delay the inevitable, if you will.

The inevitable?

The coming necessities following her birth were left unsaid, but the truth of it festered in the backs of the brains of the people the way an overhead fluorescent does months before it finally flickers out all the way and dies, buzzing louder by the day, growing insipid, breeding anger in those trapped beneath it, anger of imagined, unsaid things. From this festering, simple tasks nudged the world closer toward its end.

The—

Let me finish. This Sister hoped her silence would delay things. Or so it's been speculated.

The world didn't end.

No, not a complete end, just an end of this, I say, pointing to everything and nothing. An end to all that you know, and when all you know will amount to how long you will last when the rules no longer exist, you quickly realize you know nothing. But you better take notes. Or else.

I'm not some blank slate.

Oh? I'll tell you this as a word of warning: It's best to learn some new tricks—no matter how old the dog, I say, squeezing the steering wheel hard enough to free the air from the joints in my fingers, the knuckles too, loud enough to be heard over the grumbling engine.

But I exist. I was born after. The world did not end.

You exist for another reason, the same as me. Have they told you? Everything?

Everything? Why I exist? Because my parents—

Do you know your parents?

Yeah.

Yeah, so your parents are not they. Your parents have nothing to do with you being here right here and right now with your ass planted in my passenger seat. He stays quiet, listens, lets the last sentence hang in the air, rattle around in his head for a minute or two. Then I say, I mean the details of your employment. Have they explained the details of your employment? Do you understand what this vocation is? What all it entails?

I am to do what you do.

You are to watch and learn and take note of what I do. You will *do* nothing. You are my shadow—nothing more. Until someone tells me otherwise. Don't get ahead of yourself. Let me explain how I got this job, okay? How I've managed to keep this job, okay? I say, pointing us west where the next pick up waits.

He shifts to the left then the right, searches for some semblance of comfort in the flattened foam of the passenger seat. I imagine that seat's older than you, I say. Shift all you want, nothing'll make it any better. You're wasting your time.

Where'd you get em? He says, and I watch his reflection continue to shift in the windshield.

I scavenged them out of some rich prick's Corvette after he resettled into a tower. Bucket seats have a nice contour to em.

Had. You were a scavenger? He asks, sliding his hand over to the lever as if contemplating letting himself out of the moving vehicle.

Yeah, right you are—*had*.

You were saying? He says, letting go a long, slow breath.

Oh, right. I was welcoming the new millennia.

I waited most of my adolescent years for that evening to come to pass. All of us were. I mean, a song was even penned for the occasion. You probably don't even know it, the words: *two thousand zero zero party over, oops, out of time—so tonight I'm gonna party like it's nineteen ninety-nine.*

I know that song. It was sung by the Prince.

No, no no no.

What?

Look, there was the Queen of Soul, the King of Rock 'n' Roll, the King of Pop, and we had Prince, just Prince. He wasn't *the* Prince—but he was ours. Our Prince. Make sense?

No.

Well, it's unimportant to you, obviously. Unfortunately. But to my story, that song is integral, understand?

Hmm?

I began the evening celebrating with my best friend since junior high school. Later on that night we were joined by the woman who would become my wife. But, unfortunately, the three of us started out by eating some 15¢ chicken wings, which I dare speculate were ill-prepared. Hindsight and all, you know? Or maybe that's foreshadowing.

15¢ chicken wings?

Yeah. Why?

Sounds like bullshit.

Bullshit?

Yeah, bullshit. A chicken costs a weeks' salary,

and to eat just the wings...no one would dare be so wasteful. No one.

I laugh. Back then, my friend, back then a whole chicken, roasted and ready to go, was not even an hours' salary and people could raise them in the backyard.

Bullshit.

Okay, go ask your parents then.

I'm orphaned—the same as you.

Okay, keep saying bullshit, or maybe you could suspend your disbelief of this one little detail long enough for me to tell you how I learned I was a Carrier. Okay?

Okay. Tell me your chicken story.

You're a mouthy little fuck, huh? That's good, shows some mental acuity. That'll keep you alive out here. Anyway. By ten o'clock that New Year's Eve, both my best friend and my future wife got sick. Violently ill, in fact. It curtailed the events of the evening to say the very least. So much so that I found myself at home on the couch in plenty of time to watch the ball drop on television. I listened to the crowd and host count the seconds down until midnight between the sound of my soon-to-be wife's retching punctuated with her explosive diarrhea. That kept on until a time I became convinced there couldn't be anything left to expel, so I turned on the shower to rain down on her.

Disgusting.

You think? I could not put the smell into words if I tried.

No? Verbose as you are?

Oh, no. God, no. I could smell her all the way in the living room. I ran her a shower to help clean her up and hoped to catch the rest of the New Year's Eve special. Yet I couldn't have been more foolish going in there.

And what makes you say that?

Well, to start, I can still hear her howling for me to get up and bring her this or that or the other thing, saying, *Jaw-gnaw-thin!* I wound up missing the headliner between tending to her and succumbing to my own sympathetic puking, which I first took as a sign of my following suit with whatever sickness took hold of those two, but the food poisoning had no effect on me. Man, you don't know love until you've shared the same puke bucket with someone.

In sickness and in health. Ain't that how it's supposed to go?

Yup. Til death do you part.

Sorry.

It's all right. You know. Don't worry about it. It's one of those things. I've gotten over it as much as I'm ever going to. But, anyway, by two o'clock that morning, I think I'd seen the newscaster announce the arrival of our Baby New Year for the fifth time.

Wait. What? Why would they do that?

Do what?

Announce the Baby New Year? Did they want a mob to seize the hospital or some shit?

Back then the continent's population numbers weren't scrolled in the corner of the screen to remind the viewer of the imperfect balance. Nor did people didn't get worked into a frenzy when the number flickered and came back with a higher population count. It wasn't an implication to start thinning others out. Not back then it wasn't. No more than the hospital's billboard along the highway boasting the number of bundles of joy delivered to date.

Wait. That's what that is? I mean, I know the sign you are talking about. The one with the mother holding a child. There's something written on it, but it's been illegible my entire life.

You've been taught to read then?

Yes, I told you I've memorized the preparation manuals.

That tells me nothing. They've been aired over the Public Broadcasting Service since I was forty. The manuals haven't been printed since I was at least fifty. Not that the billboard can be read anymore. The sun and the blowing grit and the smog and the blizzards have eaten away the majority of the sign. You can barely see the child in its mother's arms, let alone make out the tale of success turned excess.

What was the purpose of it then?

Once the digital display wasn't meant to loom

overhead as a reminder to young people how abstinence is best for societal balance, rather it was a means of welcoming expectant mothers to their birthing ward and away from the private practices.

Private practices? You mea—

I mean doctors who operated outside the oversight of the Sisters. The end of that didn't come into existence until after my grandchildren.

After? They've transitioned?

Yes. The last one was unable to be born, actually. Don't worry, at some point, you'll be the next person on earth to die, I say, and grip the cracked steering wheel cover, twisting it, breaking another of the dried leather braids in doing so. He stays quiet, holds his tongue until we clear the next intersection, let's me check behind us. The cracked glass of the side view mirror makes a mosaic of everything on the road behind me and a kaleidoscope of the lines this life has left on my face.

CUT IT OUT

Shall we begin?

As if we've time to waste.

There's no need for that right now.

Yes, let's get on with it. Sister, if you would please.

Our help is in the name of the Lord who made heaven and earth. As we gather for the meeting, we call upon God to be with us. God of the Living, God of Love, Spirit of Understanding, Creator of the Universe, You are the giver of all good gifts. Praise God for past favors. We thank You and praise You for Your goodness to us. Please be with us as we discuss end of life issues. We ask this through Christ our Lord. Amen.

Amen.

Thank you, Sister.

Yes, thank you.

Why've we been called here? We have a quarterly meeting in two weeks' time.

Oh, could you be any more coy?

Hmm?

Are you actually insinuating you've somehow unplugged yourself from the rest of the populace to the point you're clueless as to current events?

Are you done?

No. You cannot be as naïve as you portray yourself. And if you are so uninformed then resign before you're removed.

You cannot remove me, we all have equal holdings.

Be quiet. The both of you. We don't have time for this nonsense right now.

Here is not the place. Let's get to it, shall we?

Here is not the place? Where else would we discuss our business?

Now who's the naïve one?

Alright! That *is* enough.

What can we possibly hope to accomplish? Not everyone needs to be here, obviously. This is nothing more than damage control at this poin—

No, everyone needs to get a clear view of the big picture.

What is the ideal outcome here? We're deemed heroes for fixing a problem we've created? We have a billion fingers pointed at us now.

Ten.

What's that now? Speak up if you're going to interrupt.

Ten billion. There's ten billion citizens pointing their fingers our way, wagging them in disapproval and blame. That's why we're here, since the question was put to the room—in case the gravity of the meeting escapes your grasp.

You think—

If the shoe fits.

You think they'll take to the streets? The people of this district are as calm as Hindu cows.

Oh, c'mon. we're not the only consortium caring for citizens. None of them knows who owns what or who's paying their physicians and pharmacists. We've nothing to worry about. Let's go home. They'll quiet down soon enough.

Whatever noise they make is not the issue here. Morale is not our concern. Get that off the table right now.

Enough, save the sidebars. We need to discuss recent events.

You mean the child. Just say it.

The child, yes, of course, the child. What else?

What else is there? How could you be so—?

Spit it out.

Wait—End of Life issues, Sister? Aren't we being a bit over the top, melodramatic?

Who here thinks the child is to blame?

Children are born in sin. Some more than others.

The child was born because of the successes of science.

Sister?

It's been discussed. Why have changes not already been made?

Melodramatic? Dramatic is what is needed. Dramatic and drastic.

And how many have been born since?

Dozens.

And how many have left the care of our facilities?

Infants, stillborns, SIDs or in general.

Just spit out the numbers,

Less.

Yes, much less.

What happened to being proactive?

What can be done?

Done?

Yes. What can be done to balance the numbers?

What do you expect us to do?

Balance? Balance is not what we need. We need the pathologists to be busier than the birthing unit. Is that not understood by anyone else sitting at this table? Or do we need to clear the air before we go any further?

We have protocols. We have *oaths*! Let us not forget that.

We have lenders who're growing impatient as well. Sentiment should be secondary at this juncture. We are at a point in history without precedent.

We have a responsibility to those who come to us for care.

We are here to promote Christ's ministry of

holistic healing for all human life with special concern for the poor and powerless.

Thank you, Sister, thank you. I too know the mission statement of this hospital.

If your concern is numbers, we should again discuss the matter of the major surgeries we perform just so a child can be born, and the mother may live.

Meaning?

A C-section is not major surgery. It is routine.

Routine major surgery.

Which leads to babies being born who shouldn't.

Shouldn't?

And you would rather mother and child to die, Sister?

We know the number of C-sections is growing, and we know what that's led to.

It's led to a change in evolution.

No. No. No. No. It's not evolution. People are fatter, in poorer health, unable to birth a child on their own. Without the aid of a team of medical professionals.

That is our job, our purpose. We provide that team and that aide.

These bigger, fatter children, they're just a matter of a simple fetopelvic disproportion. Modern man hasn't been on earth long enough to evolve. There are only medical miscalculations. No evolutionary steps—forward or back.

How many?

How many what?

How many Cesarean section births since the ten billionth citizen was born?

Here? Or at all of our hospitals?

All hospitals. Not just ours. Big picture, right? We—we all need to be thinking about the big picture here. What are the total numbers?

Thirty to thirty-two to thirty-five percent. Depending on whichever studies you look at.

That's not a number, is it? How many?

Close to two-hundred-thousand a day, worldwide.

How many days has it been?

Four.

Fucking hell.

That's not necessary. Apologize to the Sister.

No, an apology is not needed. I believe your outbursts are warranted.

Sister, what will the Benedictines say if we were to propose stopping some Cesarean section surgeries to birth some children?

Some? It is in God's hands who lives and who dies. It is not for men to decide. Doctors of Divinity, maybe. Maybe. Yet, men of medicine intervene every day.

To be a contributing member of the board, one must contribute. What is your answer?

I have offered my insight.

So, you're going to offer no opinion? Only

judgment? And sit there pointing out our failings? And who says the church is a redundancy?

Come again?

Notice your saints are no longer welcoming our patients or looming in the alcoves along the halls. Your seat at this table could be retired as well, Sister.

If they were to stop intervening—performing the cesareans—it would be no different than the vasectomies we don't allow in our hospitals or the tubal ligations we don't allow. All three interfere with the miracle of birth.

And?

And you may add this to the medical birthing agreement at once, in all our facilities, of course—Chicago to Boise. I will let them know this is happening. And—

And?

And you may ease the mother's suffering, of course.

Let billing and coding know, they'll know enough to notify the one-payer custodians, so the option is removed from the list of care provided.

Let the other districts know as well.

Send pigeons as well, while you're at it. Just as effective. How many children do you think have been sliced out of their mothers in the time since we've sat down? We're moving at a snail's pace here, goddamn it. Sorry, Sister.

Well, the satellites need to be alerted in that same breath.

We'll need to bring on more anesthesiologists.

That's no never mind. What'll we do with the excess labor and delivery nurses?

Start sorting out the essentials from the nonessentials.

Let the Father know he'll be performing more last rites in the coming days. He may want to request help from the diocese.

What preparations will the Benedictines require for this, administratively? Speaking in immediate terms.

We shall offer only our thoughts and prayers.

Shall we make the announcement then?

Let's.

Do we put it to a vote?

No, enough time has been dedicated to its discussion. The citizens will want to see that someone is doing something.

ST. LUCIA AND ST. MARIA PROPOSE A JOINT $1B INVESTMENT FOR DULUTH HEALTHCARE CENTERS

By Douglas Gehrki

Nov 19, 2030

DULUTH —The St. Lucia Specialty Care Complex and St. Maria Healthcare Center held a joint press conference Wednesday which outlined their plan to invest a combined $1 billion to upgrade and expand their two downtown Duluth complexes as well as their outlying community clinics.

The St. Lucia Specialty Care Complex will see $249 million worth of improvements in their downtown campus alone, said L.D. Hurst III, the healthcare center's CFO. It was not discussed if their satellite clinics would receive any updates during the press conference.

The St. Maria clinics found around the district will undergo a $125 million facelift while an estimated $675 million will go toward creating a new expanse of the downtown complex, according to Wesley Irby, a senior public relations official for the district's largest employer and health care provider.

However, these two proposed expansion projects hinge on whether the district will receive the grant money totaling $200 million in national support hinted at by Mayor Garland Jackson during his State of the District address right before the holidays. These funds are needed to install the public infrastructure upgrades necessary to accommodate the growing needs of the two healthcare centers. The completed projects are estimated to generate an additional $2 billion in new tax revenue in as little as ten years' time, which can then be invested in other districtwide improvement projects such as roads and schools as well as fund the police and fire departments for the foreseeable future. For perspective, $200 to $300 million in new construction is erected in Duluth during an average year. But the St. Lucia and St. Maria expansion projects will bolster those numbers with $1 billion in only two years' time.

Irby said St. Maria plans to swell their care facility by an approximate 985,000 square feet, yet the footprint will shrink by building up, not out.

Hurst began the press conference by unveiling St. Lucia's three-phase project — set to start in the spring of next year — which will carry a $36 million price tag. The initial phase of construction is said to prioritize renovations of their current five-story care facility that houses their main specialty care clinics. The renovation will include the centralization of their emergency care center, moving patients closer to specialists who may need to be called upon to provide life-saving care. This shuffling of the complex's layout will eliminate 300 parking stalls but also allow for the upgrading of the helipad with the option of a second one to be built later should the need arise.

The second phase will include construction of a thirteen-story 445-bed inpatient hospital tower. Hurst assured the district council their architects designed the new tower to take the convenience of pedestrians into consideration. Access to the neighboring waterfront rose garden will not be hindered, he said. In fact, their facility will be joined via skywalk to St. Maria's in order to foster "the feeling of a community of healing."

The third phase involves a proposed partnership with the district, one that will need to address rezoning the remaining area between the two medical campuses. It is their hope to be able to usher in a shared parking ramp large enough to accommodate patrons of the downtown merchants as well as the visitors of the healthcare centers. "With the expansion of the combined medical offerings of the St. Lucia Specialty Care Complex and the St. Maria Healthcare Center, it makes sense to assume people will flock to the area with family and friends in tow while they embark on their healing journey. To relieve the stress of the separation on our patient's loved ones, the construction of hotels or extended stay lodgings should be considered in further expansion projects. And to keep local money local, the West End craft merchant district should be relocated to a more centralized area," Hurst said.

Irby shared this sentiment and springboarded off Hurst's statement saying, "We would like to discuss the future possibility of another tower, an affordable place to live for our employees — much like U.S. Steel did for their workers in Morgan Park. But, again, by building up, not out. If we can do so, we believe it would help to relieve the housing strain, which everyone knows to be a growing issue as Duluth becomes more populated, and, now, more so as our two healthcare centers attract even more employees. Not only will our influx of new employees boost the tax base the district sees, but this tower will lessen traffic congestion, thus reducing the wear and tear and the frequency of road repair work which so often curbs other civil engineering projects."

Hurst wished to highlight how their two projects are more than a few new towers standing in the district's center, but "a gesture of goodwill to the people, a promise to provide state-of-the-art medical care for the community."

Irby illustrated this point, saying, "St. Maria Healthcare Center will shift our focus to provide ancillary medical care, phasing out nearly all of our specialized care clinics — or, nonessential medical practices — which will become the sole mission of the St. Lucia Specialty Care Complex. The hope here is to effectively end the competition between our two healthcare centers."

Mayor Garland Jackson thanked both the St. Maria Healthcare Center and St. Lucia Specialty Care Complex for bringing the expansion proposals before the district, saying, "These two projects will transform our district economically and structurally, without a doubt." He too assured both Hurst and Irby their proposals already have his, the Planning Commission, and the entire District Council's stamp of approval. He then ended the meeting by saying he promised to make procuring the necessary funds to complete the infrastructure upgrades the sole focus of his administration.

LAY OF THE LAND

Before you interrupted yourself, you were going on about how eating turned chicken somehow got you work as a Carrier. Please, do tell.

No, I didn't start the job for another fifteen years or so. Those were some pretty good years, looking back now. Things were good. Really good. For everyone. There was no us and them then, just we—the people.

Really? How'd things go fro—

No, that was naivety. Hindsight and all, you know. Enough people were all too happy to wear blinders and go along with what was asked of them. Before too long those who were pulling the strings became comfortable enough to do so without hiding behind the curtain. I, myself, went along without question for longer than I care to admit, or recall.

The curtain?

Metaphorically speaking. Puppetry is probably lost on anyone nowadays, though the practice is alive and well—let me assure you. *Well* wouldn't be the best way to word it, I suppose. It shouldn't be bathed in a warm light.

I get it. It's bad, a manipulative practice.

It's more than that. Puppets don't know they're being controlled, they're mindless, see. Anyway, if we could go back, this place would be unrecognizable to you.

You think so?

Absolutely. Life trudged along, evolving, metamorphosis after metamorphosis. Some things trudged too fast, seeing where it took us.

What went wrong?

The trudging turned into a trampling once enough people turned a blind eye. Or the right people did. But, in truth, I don't know. There's no one thing anyone can point to. And *they're* not too forthcoming with *their* missteps. Though, I can say ripples of mistrust turned to tidal waves without sounding too cynical or melodramatic.

Mistrust of who?

Whom?

What do you mean by whom?

Whom. And that whom is the corporations. The conglomerates.

The owners?

Not just the owners. The puppeteers.

That metaphor is not dead then?

No, not quite. Not until all us from before die. This district used to pride itself on being self-sustaining. People were craftsmen. Everything was made in the back of the shop and sold in the front. If something was not, or could not, be brought in from other districts for whatever reasons, we set out to make it for ourselves—better adapted for life as it is here. Whether it needed to better weather our winters or be upgraded and adapted to climb up and down the rocky slopes our streets were built atop.

That's how it is now, everyone has an assigned craft or trade, except for the scavengers and the pawnbrokers.

Now it is. Down here it is. Nowhere else was like that then. And people did whatever they wanted. Whether they showed aptitude, people were encouraged to pursue whatever romanticized dream that festered in their hearts.

Who'd let them?

Let them? Back then, people were allowed to fuck up their life and let to suffer the consequences alone—to sleep on the streets, if that's where it led them. We're talking long before the towers and the colony of people held inside became a cohesive, realized society of sorts.

Of sorts?

It's a copy of a copy and far from perfected. Far from symbiotic. But, it is the only way of life you've ever known, so there's no way for you to measure its authenticity or productivity. Your apple has no orange.

My what now?

Sorry. Back then, when people were urged to take on whatever pursuit their heart desired. Some would return to colleges and universities and vocational training schools two or three times throughout their lives only to end up working until their dying day to pay for the schooling. Both my grandfather and stepfather took time off from work to die. The two of them had to pay dues—actual fees—to work in their trades. That, atop taxes, left them owing more than they were worth to their employers.

What about up over the hill? What was over the hill back before? Wasn't it full of conveniences?

Chains, corporate chains mostly. And—ah—a few of the local businesses that flourished enough to compete alongside and open their own chains. Stacks of money stacked on more stacks of money. The American dream. That's what sat atop the hill. Though it always proved to be just beyond the horizon. Right out of reach for those who interpreted their right to the pursuit of happiness entirely the wrong way.

Have you been over the hill?

Not in a long time. Not since *they* abandoned the clinic for that community.

Which community?

The town of Herman.

That's where many of the owners lived, right?

At first. North of here and true north of here.

True north?

Along the lakeside. The district's grid wasn't laid down according to the compass, and even if it was, things've shifted since. People always assumed if your back was to the water and you faced the hill that right was east, and west was to the left.

It's not?

No, never was. People are too lazy. That's where the misdirection comes from. When the district was surveyed, it was done so in a series of a dozen triangular neighborhoods running along the waterfront. Mapmakers are morons for the most part. As is anyone who sketches out imaginary borderlines within a landmass. Only the pathetically self-important would do such a thing.

How else would we get around?

The maps are unnecessary.

Until today, I'd—ah—I'd agree with you. But seeing as how I've been thrust out into all this, he says, pointing past the windshield, a little guidance might go a hell of a long way.

So now you'd like to argue for their utility? You know, you trying to read a district map would be about as fruitful as me trying to translate some Sanskrit. The maps, even the ones loaded onto the scanner, they're obsolete, to say the least. But that might be the best way for me to frame it for you.

Outdated, you mean?

No, I mean obsolete. The neighborhoods are all but abandoned, have been for longer than I can remember. But, go on and use a map to find your way through the ones that aren't altogether abandoned, and you'll never find your way out of there. And no one will come looking. That'll be the last of you. Poof.

Poof? What's poof? Like I'll spontaneously combust or something?

May as well. They'll be nothing of you to find. Charred remains, maybe. If that. See, most folks only know their way around the towers and those do not even appear on a map, they're inside the shaded area of the hospital's campus. Just you pay attention to what I say, to where we go, and don't go—can't go.

Can't?

Good. You're listening. The westernmost street of each neighborhood travels up the hill and points to true north. You'll need to know this if you're ever to drive. We only go south from the hospital. People still call it west, though. If you pay attention to the slips you can judge how far you are to and from the hospital.

Ships?

Slips. The slipways where the boats would dock during their maintenance cycles. They're the things that used to look like fingers pointing across the bay to Superior, back when the ships sailed in here, back when the gales only came in November. The ships out there, don't pay them any mind. They move at will. One day they're lying listed to their starboard side, the next they're slugging toward the canal with a ghost at the helm. They're nothing but another abandoned skeleton from Duluth's past.

The slips you're talking about, they're the things that look like the district's toes digging down into the sand?

Yeah, except it is not sand.

It's topsoil and silt. Dirt, really. It was dirt. Dredging from when the shipping lanes in the harbor needed to be deepened. It's just dust now. Grime. The grit that coats everything once the winds stop.

And the bridge.

What about it?

Will we cross the bridge?

No, there's no need.

Why's that?

There's no need to, that's all I know. I go out and back, over and again. I don't do anything extra or just because or because boredom sets in. If you're bored out here, you're not paying attention. Once your mind starts to wander, you're done for.

Noted. So, the district crumbled and got condensed because of the weather somehow?

Is that what you think I said?

Well, no.

No is right. The causality lies elsewhere, but it was in the same stack of dominoes.

That was symbiotic then?

Parasitic is the word you're looking for.

You mean to tell me bugs did all this?

I laugh. He blinks and stares out the window and waits for me to spell it out for him.

Parasitic conglomerations.

Like a flock of locusts?

Exactly. Someone in the Capitol once decided corporations are a people—on paper, at least. And that was when things crumbled.

Meaning?

Meaning they were no longer faceless entities lingering in towering high-rises, or deities you paid tribute to with each paycheck who claimed true ownership to everything you called your own. See, once they were given the rights of a regular person, they lost their facelessness. Their ambiguity. Once they were given a face, people knew who to hate. And they weren't so fearful anymore. People could make caricatures of them—make light of them.

And just how did you come to this notion of yours?

Oh, seeing is believing. Has no one ever told you that?

My apples have no oranges, remember?

True. I watched it happen.

Ah, okay. With which owners?

The owners. The ones you're working for, for starters.

The hospital?

Yeah, the hospital. *They* were the cause of the first division.

What happened?

Nothing *happened*. People just realized things. I realized things.

Like?

Patients were not patients in *their* eyes, but consumers instead. Customers. But the customers slowly caught on how no one was getting better. They'd go to the hospital sick where they either died or became sick with something else entirely. Whatever was ailing people was almost always oddly undiagnosable, yet always treatable.

Somethings are incurable. That's just fact.

Yeah, but *they'd* pump you full of whatever until there was nothing left to siphon from your bank accounts. They'd leave you and yours bankrupt.

So, you're saying they put a price tag on a life? How'd they arrive at a price?

How? How much you got in your pocket? That's how much you're worth. There needs to be a mutualism between healthcare patient and healthcare provider for a sustainable symbiosis to exist. Without it, something else takes root: mistrust on one side, and lack of patronage on the other.

Seems bleeding you to death isn't as much of a metaphor as a blueprint.

Nope. If *they* couldn't help you at the hospital, there was no sense for you to stay there. There are only so many beds, you know? That's how come home hospice became the primary protocol for physicians to follow.

That's where people went to transition originally, right? Or am I mistaken?

No, that's how it went. Until their dying dollar, that's where the expression originated.

Okay, so if they helped and comforted the ailing, why the division?

Trust.

Trust? In general, or—

Trust in community.

Trust in the towers?

The towers were still being sketched out by their architects when this all started. No, the district was what, one hundred thousand people when you were born?

Close. I guess. I don't know.

The hospital employed about twenty thousand people back then. Give or take. I worked as a courier for the hospitals, but I didn't work at the hospitals— we were brought in later. I was, at least.

What occupies the emptied clinics then?

Who.

Okay, whom then?

The ones who have it in their heads how they need to be above it all. They're the omniscient ones here.

The puppeteers you told me about?

It's a safe bet they're up there. They know the

truth about the innerworkings of a melting pot: everything on the bottom gets burned, and all the scum floats to the top. Get it?

Kind of.

Well, curiosity killed the cat. Ever heard that one?

I have.

Think of curiosity as the people once they started to ask questions.

And the cat would be a fat cat of the corporate type in this analogy?

Now you're getting it. So they've diversified, spread themselves out, but haven't left themselves vulnerable, see? And like all corporations, the hospital has chains, branches, satellites, almost like franchises—but they all operate in accordance with the Sisters' oversight. When the Sisters partnered with whatever corporation they did to usher in a new means of management and attempt to restore a healthy societal balance, they stepped back from the day-to-day but kept a seat at the table.

Like, on the board of directors?

Exactly that. The Sisters sit at the head of that table. They are like the spirit of the law. Law, meaning: medical ethics and Hippocratic principles. Though merely in spirit. They are able to say anything that happens within their hospital walls is their god's will. The others, the hospital clinical and financial directors, became a corporate entity. And I say entity because back when the changeover began it'd been ruled that a medical conglomeration couldn't be viewed as an individual, even their chief executive. The providers, however, were given personage.

That was a good thing, yeah?

Seems so. But, at the same time, it could be argued it was all sleight of hand. That's my own cynicism oozing through, mind you. I'm not in a place to see the whole picture, now am I?

A trick then?

The time since has made it seem more of a shell game. The corporation did nothing rash. It was subtle. The first change took me months to catch. Then when I figured my eyes weren't deceiving me and my boredom hadn't caused me to make more of the world around me than what was actually there, I started asking questions.

Such as?

Hold on, I'll get there. You aren't going anywhere anytime soon, are you?

He doesn't offer an answer.

See, I began my day by picking up supplies from the main lab and distributing them to the satellite labs all around the district, over the bridge too.

We still do that?

Hold on. I'm telling you all this so I know you'll know. If I show you, let you follow me in and out of these buildings and have you watch while I go about things, you won't remember half of what to do. The mind—wanders. Got it?

Okay, yeah, I'm listening.

Good. If I arrived too early, I'd have to wait until I could scan into the supply room. If I did scan-in too early and left before all the supplies arrived, I'd be reprimanded.

How so?

Financially. A sliver of a percentage off my check. When traffic was light, I'd sit outside the entrance and watch the parade of nurses and nurse's assistants and medical assistants—or whoever—pour into the hospital. Some wore pink, some wore purple, some wore yellow, some wore green, some wore red, some would have polka dots and designs. But they'd rarely match tops and bottoms. They'd wear whatever. Mix and match.

They were allowed? Allowed to have uniforms like that?

Scrubs, I say, correcting him. And, yes, they were.

We don't wear them.

No, we never have.

Why not?

Fuck if I know. Best guess is that no one wears them outside the buildings. And outside is where we spend most of our time.

Wouldn't it be easier for them to wear them all the time? I mean, the towers are right alongside the hospital. Hell, it's all connected through the skywalks too.

No one wants others to know whether they're essential. I think that's why it took so long for me to notice. The change came in January, I later learned.

Winter.

Yes, when we had discernable summers and winters—months apart, rather than pressure systems that change the weather from one season to the next from one afternoon to the next and back again before the weeks' end. Winter, how I miss a proper winter.

Months upon months of green and white must have been something to see.

Months upon months of white, with a month or two of green, bookended by months of browns and gray.

You should have written travel brochures.

Thanks. Poetry is a passion of mine.

That's not what I meant.

I know. As I was saying before I so rudely interrupted myself again.

What? He laughs. Fucking delayed echo in here, aye?

I laugh. They all wore coats, and some wore layers, so you couldn't see what color scrubs they wore. Spring came, and I noticed the colors: royal blue, navy blue, ceil, Caribbean blue, purple, crimson, cherry red, brown, black, olive green, hunter green, slate gray, there was no mixing and matching of colors, save those who kept the hospital sanitary—they wore black bottoms and slate gray tops. A walking contradiction. Black, like those of the highest on the food chain, and gray, those whose specialized treatments were quickly deemed a luxury and an elective, rather than something necessary. Or nonessential, to use a bit of *their* own language.

Therapy was a viable treatment once?

Yeah. Specialized treatments were the bread and butter of the hospital's caregiving. Were. But that went the way of the dodo. Things changed. Even the patients wore colors coordinated to what they were being treated for and who was caring for them. Their robes were pinstriped different shades of blues and reds and greens, and gray as well, of course.

That does make good sense if you think about it.

Yeah, or it's a lot like shelving and prioritizing people. But that's not what made me question things, whether things had changed. Questions didn't burrow their way into my brain until I noticed little clusters of the same colors in the cafeteria, coming into the hospital in herds—rather than sprinklings of different colors at different times. The same colors sat together as they ate, while they smoked, and swarmed in different areas of the hospital, but never wandered to other areas—except those dressed in head-to-

toe slate gray. They moved about with an ambiguity. They seemed to be assigned everywhere and nowhere. They took patients from one corridor of the hospital to another to provide their own specialized treatments but spoke to no one while doing so. If ever they noticed me looking their way, trying to figure out just who they were, they'd cast their eyes elsewhere.

They looked down on Carriers then?

Don't know. I could never tell if they were thinking I was the shit stain or they were. Sometimes they used gurneys to move the invalid, other times they walked alongside their patients—clutching them either by the elbow or a belt tethered around the waistline.

I stopped seeing those dressed in the slate gray scrubs, or *they* stopped dressing people in slate gray, or those dressed in slate gray were deemed nonessential after the citizen was born.

You asked questions, you said.

Yes, I did.

Who'd you ask?

Those in the testing laboratories. The women in black.

INITIAL CONFIRMATION

You're here already, aren't ya?

Yeah, sorry. Didn't mean to surprise you. I try to show up exactly on time.

No, you're okay, I wasn't paying attention is all. Giving ya a little grief. Gonna get a smile out of ya yet. You watch.

I have time. Traffic was light coming up the hill. I don't imagine that'll change for a while. I didn't even get to eat anything—I didn't come up on a single red light the whole way. I guess I could have checked the time before I came in, it's my fault. I'll shoulder the blame on this one. I could have had something to eat out in the parking lot. Either way, I wanted to let you know I'm here.

Yeah, sorry. We fall behind sometimes. Most times, she says, half cringing, half smiling in a weird sort of apologetic way—most likely a photo negative of whatever is plastered across my face. I'll get it ready to travel. There's two for the incubator, one in the fridge, nothing in the freezer this time, five room temp.

Thanks, I'll put my bag down and go grab whatever is headed to the correspondence center. Do you have anything?

Nope. Not for this trip.

Back in a minute.

Through the main entrance lobby, down the stairs, through the mental health lobby, behind the desk, through two steel doors, awaits a bucket of envelopes. Those envelopes get stuffed into a waxed canvas bag which gets padlocked by me, and, of course, I don't have the key. If I was a betting man, I'd say someone sitting inside one of the cubicles does. Either the very first one or somewhere way in the back. Regardless, no one ever says a word while I'm in the room. It stays silent, save the sound of fingertips hammering away on keyboards coming from a dozen and a half different cubicles. The sound is something like the desperate click-click-clicking of beetles fucking in an attempt to save their species from the inevitable mass extinction coming courtesy of the forecasted drought which we've been told will ignore the normative morning mists and fall fog so synonymous with the northern shore of the greatest of the Great Lakes. The bag then goes inside another bucket, one with flaps, which get folded and sealed with serialized zip-ties. It's the arc of the covenant, or so it would seem. All this, down the hallway, through the main entrance lobby, down the stairs, through the two steel doors, stuffing, padlocking, zip-tying, back through the two doors, back through the mental health lobby, back up the stairs, back through the main entrance lobby, back down the hallway and into the lab, takes all of forty-five seconds.

Just you today?

Umm...let's see. There's me, one for training, one at lunch, so there'll be three of us on your next pick up. Unless one of us can fit in a break.

Where's the one who always wears the purple scrubs with the Norseman pattern?

Blonde?

Yeah. AD...J, I think.

They transferred her to the community clinic on the east end of the hillside.

Oh. Are the rest of you wearing black in mourning?

No, we—*they*—we have to wear black now. All lab technicians at all the clinics. And the main lab at the hospital. We can wear the white lab coats, too.

Like the doctors?

Doctors are to wear business professional attire with the new clothing policy put out by the new owners. No lab coats or scrubs for the doctors unless they're surgeons.

Gotcha. Chained to the radiator. I never see you at any of my other stops. You're in charge here, right?

No. No one is really in charge anywhere. I am senior to some of the other technicians who float here, I'm just the one who can't leave. I'm assigned here.

Gotcha. If that's everything, can I get your initials on here?

Yeah, of course. Anyone can sign, by the way. Anyone wearing black, not just me.

Okay, thanks. That'll help me get out of here faster. You know, the whole time I've been at this job, I've been waiting for you to be free so I can check out of the clinic.

What's your name? You've been driving for four months now, right? Most don't last that long. You sticking around?

For now.

What's your name?

Shaddox.

Oh, you're military, she smiles. My husband still does that sometimes.

Yeah, I was. Sorry. Old habit. I'm Jonathan. My name's Jonathan, I mean.

500 NONESSENTIALS HAVE VOLUNTEERED SINCE THE RIGHT-TO-DIE LAW CAME TO FRUITION

By Bryn Efurd
June 15, 2043

DALLAS — More than 500 nonessential citizens took their own lives with the assistance of a lethal cocktail of prescription pharmaceuticals in the first six months since the right-to-die law came into effect nationwide. The law states the terminally ill are able to request life-ending treatments from their district hospital if it is agreed upon by two or more physicians that the patient has less than a year to live.

The End of Life Option Act — co-sponsored by the Benedictine Sisters

— has made every district hospital in the North American territories able to aid in end-of-life procedures, as long as it is overseen by and administered in their facilities, to include the satellite clinics located in the sub-urban fringes.

To date, a vast majority of the nonessentials who have volunteered mirror what is seen across the districts in the European continent, which was the first union to legalize the practice nearly five decades ago. Though the North American territories are far more diverse, the bulk of those who have volunteered are of quantifiable European ancestry, university educated, greater than 50 years of age, and proliferated with malignancies.

Physician-assisted deaths accounted for only three out of every 35,000 deaths in the North American territories between January and June of this year, according to the National Bureau of Census. This number is much lower than anticipated when the law was first introduced in 2041, however, these relatively low numbers have not quelled the debate as to whether empowering doctors to dispense the drugs is an ethical medical practice.

Representatives who introduced and sponsored the law have released findings which claim only 512 of the 731 prescriptions were administered, as of the end of May. Whether the patients transitioned unexpectedly or decided against the procedure, is not known.

"Many citizens maintain lifelong faith-based values and beliefs concerning just what makes a life worthwhile. They too seek the assurance that when their health worsens, and more than preventative health care is needed — just as with the onset of the pain associated with their aging and their eventual dying — they won't have to suffer through it," said Dr. Joseph Mertins, a psychiatrist and professor at the Superior University. "Too, they admit wanting to be able to have the option to say how they're going to spend their remaining time," Dr. Mertins continued. "It's an exit strategy which will relieve their family nucleus of the burden, really."

Raylene Day, an attorney with the Citizens First Foundation and opponent of the End of Life Option Act, said "The law has effectively normalized physician-assisted suicide. The issue taken with this is that there really is no way for anyone to know for certain if a nonessential citizen was what we consider to be a consenting individual when taking this cocktail." She punctuated her point by saying, "The tragedy here is how doctors are aiding ailing nonessential patients by giving them what is assumed to be nothing more than a fistful of painkillers along with a fistful of sleeping pills, and then leaving them for the orderlies to deal with," in reaction to hearing the numbers of volunteers released two weeks ago.

Patrick Cawein, a spokesman for the national governance said "The low percentage of volunteers in the last half year isn't surprising considering citizens are still learning about the End of Life Option Act. The entire first year when Europe initially began the procedure, there was only 105 physician-assisted terminations, though the number has reportedly grown to 637 as of last year."

Cawein reiterated how, under the current stipulations of the law, doctors may not initiate conversations concerning aid in self-termination with those who would fall into a nonessential category. Instead, the citizen — or an appointee, such as their family or a retained estate custodian— need to ask for the medicines unprompted.

"The districts' data shows how even during the earliest weeks after the End of Life Option Act was implemented, the law worked reasonably well with terminally ill citizens who were able to take solace in knowing there was an option available for them to end their own intolerable suffering — if they decided to so choose" said Aron Tyree of Compassionate Choices for Citizens, a group of lobbyists who pushed for the adoption of the right-to-die law across all districts in the North American territories.

The group released a report this month highlighting profiles of the 517 nonessential citizens it knew of who were prescribed the lethal cocktail of medications between January and June of this year.

The lethal combination of prescription pharmaceuticals is something of a conundrum for doctors when considering their Hippocratic Oath. Administering the procedure is voluntary for physicians and medical facilities alike, despite its current state of lawfulness as well as it now being within the patient's rights. Some faith-affiliated hospitals have not allowed their physicians to prescribe said medicines, while others argue its validity.

The Benedictine Sisters, for instance, encouraged dialogue from their physicians before they entertained any thoughts or concerns from the other controlling members of the board for their hospitals spanning from Chicago to Boise.

The conclusion they reached was "simple," they said in a recent interview. "'In second Corinthians it says, '*So to keep me from becoming conceited because of the surpassing greatness of the revelations, a thorn was given me in the flesh, a messenger of Satan to harass me, to keep me from becoming conceited.*' — We see no reason for the faithful to spend their final days within our walls suffering such an intolerable pain as that of Satan's thorn.'"

"The Benedictine Sisters have chosen to approach the issue head-on, rather than closing their eyes in prayer—praying for it to go away," President Burr said upon learning of their allowing the procedure to take place in their facilities, totaling 1/6th of all medical establishments in the North American territories.

"Nevertheless," Burr continued, "I

understand the End of Life Option Act still faces opposition from some bastions of the for-profit corporate healthcare providers. After all, it is in their shareholders best interest to treat the nonessentials as long as possible. Personally, I'd rather see them free up a hospital bed than drain a family's resources unnecessarily."

The national governance ruled earlier this spring that a suit to appeal the End of Life Option Act will be allowed to be heard at trial later sometime during this year.

An announcement has been made of a potential severance bonus to be offered to the surviving dependents of those who voluntarily self-terminate in the future.

ROAD TRIPPING

What travels with us?

Medical specimens.

That's vague.

Very much so.

You don't know?

Oh, I know.

And?

And they didn't tell you what this is, did they?

They told me my function.

Your function.

Yes, they told me my function.

Well, let's be thankful for that, shall we?

What do you mean?

Your purpose. One of the great mysteries of life—it's been answered for you. One less thing you have to think about. One less thing you have to lose sleep over.

What do you mean?

The purpose of life. The meaning of life. You're a cog, aye?

A cog? How old are you? You can't call someone a cog, you know?

You don't know what a cog is, do you? I laugh aloud.

Why don't you tell me.

Hold on. Quiet. This is one of the intersections that it'd behoove you to give your attention.

Okay.

Quiet.

Holy Fuck! Through the building?

Quiet, I growl.

The blackness brings a hush over him. The echoes of the engine amplify off the monstrous concrete walls, causing him to shrink in his seat. He looks around—and behind us—wondering if we're being followed, being chased. He doesn't understand there's a delay in his hearing the acceleration and the echo of the revving engine and the lunging that follows and pushes him even further back into his seat. Sensory deprivation is a funny, funny thing for those who think they've got a good grip on the world around them. He doesn't know any better than to go limp, just go with it. He's a fighter, so he cringes while he's thrust back into the light of day. He balls up, thinking it'll protect him. He's not ready for... any of this.

You know that big clock face on that big tower

that sits smack dab in the middle of the district's circumcenter?

The one within the first high-rise built?

Yeah. That'd be the one I'm talking about. That clock is not just a clock. It is dozens of cogs. Hundreds, I'd guess. Each one, necessary for the clock to enumerate the hours of the day. Individually those cogs are expendable, unimportant things. Without them, the clock is a relic.

Without one of the cogs wouldn't it still be a clock.

No.

You so certain?

Yes, the measure of one clock is another. They're reflections of one another.

Okay. If you say so.

Confused?

Yes.

Good. There are too many pieces of the puzzle to bother with. Concentrate on what's in front of you. Or behind you, more appropriately.

And what's behind me?

The cardboard boxes are filled with vials of blood—up to thirty-six. They get surprisingly heavy. Grab them with both hands.

Ever dropped one?

Not yet. A few have surprised me, though—given me an oh-shit moment.

What else?

The vials with the swabs inside are urine, as are the cups. The cups are obvious, I'd hope. The petri dishes could be anything—sometimes they're room temperature, sometimes you'll find big bags full of them in the incubators. They'll smell.

Stink, you mean? Why's that even worth mentioning? Everything stinks these days.

You'll never grow used to the smell of slow cooked waste and fluids.

Okay. What's in the frozen buckets?

The three small ones are stool.

Stool?

Yes, stool. Shit is stool. Bloody shit.

What makes someone shit blood?

If I ever get so sick, I'll let you know.

Can't wait.

That line about how we deliver health is a lie. We deliver sickness. The people know it, but they think the people are stupid and their slogans will keep the cogs safe. The people are smart, they're not cattle. But maybe they're right, maybe they're wrong. Still, they've forgotten how cattle can stampede and trample their herdsmen.

The big buckets I see you carrying sometimes, what are those?

Those are different. Those buckets are filled with placenta, afterbirth, lengths of umbilical cord—all the nasty shit that comes with new life.

What's that have to do with delivering sickness?

Nothing. See, the hospitals have become a place

of checks and balances. They're not centers for healthcare and healing.

They're not?

Nope. Have you ever gone in for treatments?

No.

Any of your household ever gone in for treatment?

Yes.

And?

And they were incurable.

Incurable? They couldn't restore their health? Healed what ailed them? How bout stabilized them enough to return home so they could expire surrounded by familiar faces?

No.

No is right. They haven't allowed that for a long time. Longer than you've been around. See, each of the buckets is a baby born. The pathologists want to know all they can about the children coming into this world naturally.

What about the others?

The ones who don't make it naturally? Their people bury them, I'd assume. I hope. Mother and child both.

We don't—

Oh, you think the big coolers are—no. No, the big coolers are limbs, legs, arms, feet, hands. Not fetuses. Fuck no.

No?

Fuck no.

The pathologists want those, too?

The limbs and appendages? They want to know what's making people sick, what's thinning the herd, what infections are going around. Those coolers are filled with necrotic limbs. Parts of people. Amputations. Don't worry about becoming sick from any of these samples. They're sealed up well enough. Remember, it's just your job. That's my best advice. Worry about what's in front of you instead—for right now—what could jump out in front of you. You're a messenger of death when you're in this job. Remember that. That's exactly what you are. That's all you are.

They told me something to the effect of us carrying things that cannot be sent by any other means than by hand. Or vehicle, I guess.

That would be the bins. See, what you need to understand about this vocation is how anyone who knows anything about what all it is we do has an opinion as to what it is we should prioritize, but we don't bother with all that—everything we do is of equal import, as far as we're concerned. That's why the specimens are inside a thing that's inside a thing that we put inside something else.

All right.

In that same breath, inside each of those bins is a bag and those bags are zipped and the zipper is tethered to the bag. A padlock connects the two. Inside the bag is an envelope. The envelope is clasped and glued shut. Inside the envelope are test results—positive or negative—that right there is what cannot be sent by any other means than by hand.

Messengers of death.

That's right, messengers of death, I nod. Most people who are sick or ailing know it. Or suspect it. But, still, denial grows stronger as time goes on. People protest, yet, everyone gets tested. Negative or positive translates to essential or nonessential, right?

Right.

Sometimes the donors don't want the doctors to know. They don't want to know themselves. If the doctors know, then they'll know, then the donors will be called back in for treatment. That's what the donors fear most. Not being sick but being treated.

How successful are the treatments these days?

Depends on how you'd define success, I suppose.

Everyone donates?

Everyone. Except those who live in the suburban fringes.

Those who do donate and fear finding out and fear the doctors finding out, do they try to stop you on the road sometimes? Or interfere with you bringing their donations to the testing labs?

Sometimes. You asking questions you know the answers to? Taking my focus off the road for no good reason?

No. Curious is all. Want to clarify, you know? Want to get the gravity of what I've gotten into.

Well, I wouldn't worry about it too much, if I was you. Once you're assigned a vocation, there's no getting out. You're stuck, you should know that, whether you like it or not. And as far as the reasons behind the actions of these donors you're so curious about, I can't help you a whole lot. But, the best way I've found to wrap my head around it is that these are desperate times populated with desperate people resolved to take desperate measures—because, apparently, there's something they've found worth sticking around for.

What do you say? What do you tell them? For that matter, what should I say?

I don't say anything to them.

No? Why not? You ignore them or something?

Like that little voice in the back of my head.

Your conscience, you mean?

Sure. I used to try to spend my day making sure I could sleep at night, but now there is a caplet for that.

Have you ever stopped to think ignoring them just makes things worse? Ratchet up their desperation even more so?

I don't say a word. Never have, never will. Given the opportunity, they will stop you dead in your tracks if you pause or even slow down any for them. Desperation is something to be feared, it's more powerful than hate. No one wants to be deemed nonessential.

So you don't stop?

I didn't bolt the v-plow onto the front of this vehicle. But I'm thankful every single, solitary day that someone decided to, you know?

So, fuck em? Keep on going. Drive on.

Mmmhmm. I don't know what all their intentions are, or their level of commitment. But I do know what an ambush looks like.

Ambush? Little paranoid, are we?

But I don't intend to find out. I do like a good mystery, you know? Some questions don't really need answers.

Has anyone ever stepped out in front of you, urged you to stop? Begged?

No one ever steps out in front of a Carrier.

Never? Not once?

They leap. Those who decide to do something of the sort, they commit. They never stand in the roadway, waiting. And while you're mulling this all over, let me interject this little nugget of hard-earned wisdom.

What's that?

Don't ever swerve out of the way of a pedestrian.

No?

Fuck no. Accelerate.

How do you know whether they're patients or donors, or someone out and about scavenging? Or, for that matter, how would they have any clue about you being the Carrier?

I don't imagine you've seen a Scavenger out scouring the sub-urban fringes, but I'll guarantee you'll never see a sickly one either. See, you're just along for the ride right now. You can't comprehend how hypervigilance can become someone's default setting, huh?

What do you mean?

Well, you did ask the question, and it does deserve an answer. So, let me be clear about this. I see them waiting in the hospitals, donating in the labs. I see them arrive at the satellites with greater frequency. Their faces become more familiar over time. They'll appear on days when the pharmaceuticals are shipped as well. Those ones tend to stick out more so than the others. They've got a mix of emotions twisting up their face when they see you. And they do see you. They're waiting to see you so they can see their physician. The first time I saw someone I once worked with—a co-worker from long before I went to war—I wanted to acknowledge him, be a friendly face from an earlier lifetime, but we are to be shadows and not interact with donors. Policy. We are to scan in and out of the laboratories as quick as we can. But, still, the donors notice you no matter how fast you move or how much you try to remain a shadow in their periphery. None of them walk into the donation areas acting aloof, or anything other than vulnerable. They're on the highest alert level you could imagine. They're watching everything that's happening, trying to figure out what the women in black are about to do to them. Their eyes'll lift when you come through the doors and leave with their vials. And they sure as shit do not blink one iota while you're in there.

They watch you?

Everyone watches you when this is your vocation. They don't see you, they see a cog. And you will watch them and notice them change. Going back to that co-worker of mine, it was his expression that grabbed my attention. Expression. Singular. His wife brought him and kept him talking while he waited, but no matter the discussion his face never changed. Then his face thinned. Then he wasn't there. Then I saw him dangling from an overpass along this route, naked, a husk, hanged by the neck with the robe he wore during his treatments for his respiratory therapy: white with brown pinstripes. He made sure someone from the hospital saw him, not as a nonessential but as a man with a voice, one who could still choose things for himself.

You didn't stop for him with him swinging in the wind?

No, you never stop, never slow, never swerve. Just go. Accelerate. Got it?

Just do the job, fuck people?

Apathy is key. Apathy will save your soul. And your life.

Forgive me if I disagree.

Oh, you're going to get all quiet on me now, aren't you? That's good. It's good to be a thinking man. But don't get too deep inside yourself. All that mess about *never* stop or slow or swerve—it's bullshit.

Bullshit?

Yeah, remember this, it'll serve you in the future. Any time you come across a hard and fast, black and white, rule, something brought it about. It's not something someone just made up for shits and giggles.

I'd assume so.

There was this donor at a lab. He was sick, carrying a contagion of some sort. No lab or doctor or test was needed. Everyone knew, just by looking at him. He knew, too. They didn't know, not yet, but they'd know soon enough. You could see he was fevered, stupefied. His donation was completed while I was attempting to gain a signature and leave for the hospital, but the one I told you about who could never leave the lab asked me to wait and bring it then. She said it was temperature and time specific. Always listen for them to throw that term around. When they say that, you have to take it right then and there and make the time up on the road. Destroyed or unusable donations become your fault—each one is a percentage taken from your remittance, so you wait.

Makes sense.

When I left, he followed. He beckoned me to stop before I made the doors, but as is our practice—our policy—I did not interact or engage with him, a donor. Nevertheless, he persisted. And pursued me.

He followed you to the hospital?

I stayed ahead of him most of the way into the district, but the streets narrow the closer you get to the circumcenter.

Darker too, the sunlight is all but choked out the closer you get. Bout black as night. All day long, sun up to sundown.

Exactly. I couldn't see him, but I could hear the whining engine of his motorbike over my own engine. I hoped they would intervene, but it was of no use. I would have been happy to see some overzealous scavenger decide they wanted his bike bad enough to take him off the road.

How'd he tried to stop you?

Shot at me—with something.

Tried to gun you down? That wasn't mentioned in the training video.

The bullets did little more damage to the back doors and windows than a hailstorm might. Though, when I realized I wasn't sure how far back he was, just that it wasn't far, I locked my brakes up and waited for him to close the distance. From what I could tell, the handlebars and front forks of the motorbike broke free from the frame and he flipped over the handlebars. The hand he held the throttle with wrapped around the whole works, breaking his arm in more places than I could count.

He died?

He was at full throttle. It seems the trauma of the impact caused his body to seize, to clench every muscle, including the ones controlling the fingers clasped onto the gun. His somersaulting over the handlebars put him in the perfect position to send a burst of bullets straight into his brain. What was left of him and the handlebars wedged their way between my backdoors and bumper. I can't really say how long he traveled with me, but everything south of the pelvis was gone when I got to the testing laboratories.

IT'S JUST ME

There're how many Carriers then?

Just me.

In the entire district of Duluth, you're the only Carrier running around to all the satellites and hospice homes?

Yeah, now. It wasn't always this way. It came about gradually, see. Nowadays those who transport donations are just Runners.

And me, he says, waving a hand in my periphery. Don't forget about me.

Am I training you, or are you watching me?

I'm your shadow, remember?

A shadow, kind of there and always falling behind.

I'm new.

I am entirely well aware.

When do you go home? Fuckin sleep?

Gah—a crackling dispatch will wake you quick enough. And I do go home. But it's more quiet behind the wheel than at home.

So you just park and close your eyes somewhere?

Sometimes I do.

Go home, old man.

Those three-foot-thick walls aren't nearly thick enough, you know. And sleep? Sleep is for the weary. Isn't that how the saying goes? When was the last time you got some good sleep, youngin? Never. Fuckin never. Not if you were born into this.

This? This is all I've ever known. I sleep fine.

Fine—that's exactly it. Sleeping fine is all you've ever known.

I read somewhere how a lack of sleep can make some people irritable. Irrational even. Hallucinatory, if it goes on long enough.

That's good. Reading's good for you.

Pamphlets at the hospital can provide one with clarity.

Clar—clarity? Books are where you'll find clarity. Novels, older than you, is where you'll find clarity. Medical informational pamphlets, I think not.

All right, all right. Shit.

Anything written since you've been born is written with a slant, so to speak. But, you, you were something of a surprise. Clarity? No one said you'd be riding with me.

And yet, ta-dah!

You sure you're not to be a Runner? And stay one?

You sure you're going to be doing this much longer? How much more can you soldier on?

Time'll tell, huh?

There are no more routes, right? Just dispatches.

Other than what I do? Basically. There are no more set loops anymore. Not like there used to be. But I stay on the move for most of the day. If I can manage, that is. Still, you need to know where it is you're going. And where not to tread. And tread lightly wherever you do go.

Tread lightly in this big metal mother fucker?

This big metal mother fucker has a finesse unto itself which you lack the life experience and imagination to wrap your head around. Give it time, and you'll see. That is, if you're taking my vocation for yourself. If that is what you intend to do. Or what *they* intend to have you do.

Interesting. Interesting.

What is?

I mean. Umm, do you read the highway marquees anymore?

I keep my eyes on the road.

Unless there's a sandstorm brewing or a blizzard kicking up or they think the gales are going to make it up this high again, you know what—do you know what it says? It says:

DONATE BLOOD THE RIGHT WAY. NOT ON THE HIGHWAY

Good advice.

They mean you. It's meant to warn people to stay

away from you, to let you be, to not try to interfere, to just let you do your job.

Ha-ha! *Move, bitch—get out the way, get out the way!*

Shit, he whispers.

What? Really? It doesn't do you any good to whisper when you're two feet from me. If that, I add and swipe my hand toward his head.

Have you ever seen your face when you sing those lyrics? Looked in the mirror? Caught your reflection one way or another? Hmm? Have you?

Nope.

You are *not* well.

I am a man of the times.

What's that supposed to mean? You saying you think I'm—what, that I'm ill-suited for the here and now? I was born into this. Did you forget that? If either of us fits the mold, it's me. You're the one who had to adapt.

Indeed, indeed. You have a point. But consider this, because you were born into this, as you've said, you lack any outside perspective. And you are right. I am not well. We're all a little mad here.

I'm mad? You're mad. Why're you grinning like that? That's the happiest I've seen you. It's un-fucking-nerving.

FEWER BIRTHS THAN DEATHS IN MAJORITY OF THE NORTH AMERICAN DISTRICTS

By Oliver Aist
August 11, 2040

CHICAGO — Deaths reportedly outnumber births in more than 90% of the districts in the North American territories demographers have found, warning of what could be a faster than anticipated transition to a future in which those who come into this world naturally outnumber those who would otherwise need medical care to see them through until the end of what is considered to be their tender years.

The National Bureau of Census projects the number of essential citizens will drop below 25% before

2045. But a new independent report asserts that people are dying faster than they are being born in 7 districts, up from 4 just two years earlier — some other demographers speculate the shift may come even sooner.

"The societal balance came and went faster than we anticipated," said Orin D. Seright, a demographer, and co-author of a report which examines the period from 2033 to 2038 using data from the Chicago District Center for Essential Statistics, the national agency that tracks natural births and deaths. He admitted he was so astounded with the findings at first that he petitioned to examine the original documents used to build the digital database which was compiled after the last election season.

The pattern began nearly two decades ago, immediately following the birth of the 10 billionth citizen, in a handful of districts home to a largely aging populace. Another report shows how fertility rates plummeted after the sub-urban fringe-dwellers were relocated to district propers around the time of the abolishment of abortions, cesarean section surgeries, vasectomies, and all other medical corrections and impediments of the human reproductive system. These compounded factors have put the demographic change on an even faster track than initially projected. Since the report's completion, both Boise and Denver have been added to the list of districts where deaths outnumber births.

Demographers warn this change has sweeping implications for identity claims as well as the continent's unilateral political and socioeconomic status, transforming a once mostly European-descended society into a multiethnic and ultimately ambiguous racial patchwork made of Indigenous, African, Hmong, and Yucatan-descended peoples. The overwhelming majority of the youngest North Americans are now of non-European ancestry and appear less like older generations than at any point in history, resulting in the need to test blood quantum for ethnicities of each individual person who makes it to adulthood within the North American territories. In the Olympia district alone, 86% of children have at least one non-European-descended parent, Professor Seright said.

Further solidification of demography's march forward followed the last election season when the National Bureau of Census released population estimates indicating a decline in sub-urban fringe-dwelling populations. Although the drop is small, just 0.07% or 81,713 abandoned sub-urban dwellings since the last election season. But a demographer from the National Bureau of Census, Linda Gideon, stated it follows a 7,640 occupancy drop from the year before, one so insignificant it was largely believed a likely sign of nomadic and undocumentable resettlements.

What do these shifts mean for future district maps? Some experts argue rapid demographic changes are to blame for the end of multilateralism upon the North American continent and drove European-descended voters to support Geoff Burr in the final voluntary election.

Of the districts where deaths exceed births, eight voted for Mr. Burr and eight voted for Ruth Sentman. Four districts flipped political leanings since President Geneva Puryear in 2034 to Mr. Burr in 2038 — Cleveland, Detroit, Philadelphia, and Atlanta. It is no longer clear how or if the demographic change will affect political change in the coming years with Mr. Burr's administration in place.

"It was once believed that one could manifest their destiny based upon their demographic — and with so many people of color — it has proven prophetic," said Jo Ragland, a social psychologist at Superior University. "But they also say North America will become more progressive. However, we know we cannot afford to speculate in such ways. We cannot assume European-descended voters will maintain their current political allegiances, neither can we assume the so-called people of color will work toward any coalitions."

At its most basic, a district is defined by its populace, and every district experiences this uniquely and without precedent. Atlanta, for instance, was the first district where deaths outnumbered births in 2038, largely because it became home for medical tourists during the cooler months following the submergence of the Floridian peninsula — yet its population grew faster than any other district on the continent.

Deaths began to exceed births nationwide in 2039, according to the findings. However, in many districts, as in Atlanta, the migration of European-descended people from the sub-urban fringes initially remedied the societal imbalance. However, in 13 districts, including Phoenix, Detroit, and New York, these migrations ultimately did not prove to be on a large enough scale to prevent the present imbalance, according to Graeme Barrett, a demographer at the Superior University and the report's co-author. Four other districts reported declines in their European-descended populace that same year: Olympia, Philadelphia, Denver, and Dallas.

The escalated death rate of the European-descended population began in the sub-urban fringes long before it ever took hold in the inner-districts. As of the last election season, European-descended people account for less than 3% of the continent's populace, according to blood quantum studies conducted throughout the North American territories during a collaborative study of the districts reported deceased.

"It's hard to come across people of an adolescent age in the sub-urban fringes anymore," said Jeff Johnson, 51, a former occupational therapist from the Saint Lucia medical campus in the Duluth district. Both his sons left for the Superior University last year and are yet to return — a paradigm gaining momentum for young men from the sub-urbanfringes. "It seems my generation will be the last to stay and claim their inheritance and entitlements from their parents," said Mr. Johnson.

"Fewer women healthy enough to endure natural childbirth means fewer children," Ernestine Scrape, Duluth district's superintendent of education, said. The district reports its populace at a 60% loss of school-age children since the late 2020s. Before then, the district required a dozen educational centers, she said. Soon it will require only three.

The district is now home to what Dr. Scrape refers to as "bookended" demographics, meaning: the bulk of the populace is either over the age of 60 or under the age of 10. The prime vocationally-appointable population is minuscule comparatively.

Mr. Johnson has grown accustomed to this turn of the tide

in the culture. Still, he shared how he loved growing up in the sub-urban fringes and is thankful he was able to care for his parents after they'd grown frail in their later life. "But the North American territories are not really set up for that anymore, it seems," he added. He plans to migrate to the district of Atlanta before the coming winter season in order to live with his daughter, a pharmacist.

Demographic differences aside, European-descended resettlers — especially less educated European-descended resettlers — are speculated to make up the bulk of quantifiably verified voters in the North American territories for the foreseeable future. "Resettlers lacking a university education made up 73% of voters in the final voluntary election in 2038," said Wava Scaramuzza, a political scientist who completed an exhaustive study of demography and politics earlier this spring. University-educated resettlers accounted for approximately 17%. Mrs. Scaramuzza continued by saying "Mr. Burr's party could continue to dominate presidential elections while losing the popular vote through 2042 if they do even slightly better amongst European-descended resettlers who haven't attended university," while other voting patterns are rumored to continue to hold steady as they have for a generation.

This momentum has given politicians an incentive to emphasize the issues of forced migration and quantified ethnicity where they are most polarized by differing degrees of education. The dichotomy of the classes has grown incrementally amongst the sub-urban since the resettlement began. "In 2030, politically speaking, there seemed little difference between resettlers with university degrees and those lacking," Mrs. Scaramuzza said. Both voted for Burr over Sentman by a 20-point margin in 2038. Mrs. Sentman lost the uneducated sub-urban resettler vote by 31 points, double Mrs. Puryear's 2034 loss while carrying the university-educated resettler vote by seven points.

"This is an undeniable change in the political climate," Mrs. Scaramuzza said. "This is why Mr. Burr's party has been able to weather these demographic changes, largely courtesy of the uneducated, or undereducated, and, thus, uninformed European-descended resettler voters."

There are still some academics who argue how the shift to a European-descended resettler minority might be several more election seasons away than the numbers suggest. While the National Bureau of Census catalogs every person of multiple ethnicities as a nonresettler, some experts state this can skew the number of self-proclaimed resettlers amongst the voting populace. In the here and now, a child of a European-descended mother and Yucatanian father is cataloged as Yucatanian, even though their blood quantum shows the child to be of mixed ancestry. Said child, once of voting age, could be identified by voting officials as ambiguous and therefore as a resettler.

"In doing so, the National Bureau of Census applies a 20th-century construct of ethnic identification to an ethnic evolution of sorts, one which will never reverse or devolve, ever," Professor Seright said. The rapid rise of ambiguous ethnic blends has led to an age peopled by those whose identities are objective. Those who "act like resettlers," he said. "It's easiest if you consider them as a sort of integration of a resettled chimera."

TAKE YOUR MEDICINE

What changed?

Not a thing.

Something must have changed. Where was the plot twist? This all didn't come about because a baby was born, and the music died. People didn't wake up the next morning outside their minds.

Some things did change, yes. No one thing. Circumstances breathed new life into people's survival instincts. Survival of the fittest, and whatnot. No one wanted to wait and see whether that meant them. No one. So, a sort of intelligent design—one bred from fear—began to fester among the masses. Or so to speak.

Meaning?

I mean, instead of waiting to see how things would be handled by those who handle such things, some went so far as to concluded that more people walking the planet meant less food, water, shelter, and conveniences, to go around, so, obviously, fewer people would have to mean there would be more to go around, which is much more conceivable a concept than to forego opulences and overindulgences for those who knew such luxuries. Remember, the thinning came about not because the people could not be fed, but because their appetites could not be satisfied.

And you? What did you do?

I was unbothered by it all.

Unbothered? He says back to me seemingly unconvinced. Really?

Truly. I was born into poverty. Taught to milk goats as a toddler. We kept half a dozen. Chickens too. When they stopped laying eggs they became dinner. But dinner didn't happen every night.

So, you learned to go without?

When I was in the desert wars, too, we thrived while doing more with less.

So, all this? he says, pointing to everything and nothing.

This is nothing more than a slow and steady—natural progression. One which I never once found the slightest bit jarring. I am still here, aren't I?

So it seems.

Like a cockroach.

Cockroach?

Don't worry about it. It's a big fucking bug that won't die.

But it did, or they did. Didn't they?

Perhaps they did, I tell him, and point down

toward the floorboards and beyond that the roadway and beneath that the crumbling pipes which once ushered the rushing waters of Zenith Sea to every faucet and toilet in town and beyond all that to the two hundred miles of subterranean tunnels that lurk beneath my feet shadowing the main thoroughfares of the district of Duluth, a motion that makes him lift his feet from the floorboards and dart his eyes to every darkened nook and cranny in sight– or out of sight– before he looks back to me, questioning the thing I said. Seeing said look of perplexity smeared across his face, I continue and explain to him, how it is still the meek who shall inherit the earth.

The meek shall inherit the earth. What kind of bullshit is that?

It's from the Book of Matthew. It's meant to comfort the masses.

The masses?

Yes, dwindling as they are.

Dwindling is one way to put it, yes. What pushed the dominos over in this district? People couldn't have just lost their minds because some baby was born. People must have seen it coming, right?

Looking back now it's safe to say, yes, some saw things. Alarmists. Though, unfortunately, they were given equal audience as the naysayers and deniers and spin doctors—two or more talking heads up on the screen hollering over one another, each given equal import by the host and viewers alike—each and every morning while people pored over the front-page headlines and did what they could to sweeten the bitterness of whatever they chose to swallow on down—coffee or tea or a slew of pharmaceuticals, both prescribed or acquired—just to make it out their front doors. But people were happy, utopic. No one really pondered how what happened in capital cities or corporate headquarters could affect their individual selves.

You what now?

Utopic, I suppose the word means nothing to you, does it? Utopic, the short version is pretty much the opposite of what we have now. Life, everything, flourished. Unchecked. Then the ten-billionth citizen was born. Flash forward to three winters later when they decided how those not voluntarily vaccinated would be excused from their vocations.

Excused?

So to speak. We're just talking about the hospital workers here, not the everyday citizens. We carriers were exempt, at first. We were independent contractors, private citizens who worked for a company that provided a much-needed service for the hospital, until the day we too were thrust under the hospital's umbrella. Forcefully, I might add. No one ever asked if we wished to stay on or transfer over to work directly for them. Some of us just kind of figured it out on our own time.

There wasn't any sort of meeting or memorandum or bulletin you maybe missed?

No, they were as subtle as could be. Meet the new boss, same as the old boss. That's the attitude they were hoping we'd have, at least.

Same, eh?

Yeah, at least at first. Same shit, different pile.

And when was that again?

The best I can remember is that it was right about the third winter after the birth of the ten-billionth citizen, like I said. It was right after the start of the new fiscal year, October.

Fiscal year? You mean physical year.

No, a year is not a physical thing. What do you expect me to say, time is a construct?

Construct? How do you build time?

I'm being facetious here. It's the fiscal year I'm talking about. Look. Of the nearly ninety-some-thousand citizens who lived within the district, an approximate seventeen-thousand worked for the hospital in one way or another—either at the central campus or the varied satellites sprinkled throughout the sub-urban fringes east, north, and south, of the district. The reasoning they gave for the mandatory vaccinations was due to the hospital reaching critical manning levels because people were taking time away—too much, in their minds—citing or claiming an illness for their absence, usually one which carried a communicable contagion for a handful of days.

Different strains of influenza and such. Even the common cold could be excuse enough for someone to stay away a day or two, or three. These absences took a toll on the hospital and the satellites, so it was not much of a surprise when everyone got ninety days to comply and get their vaccinations. Reminders played hourly via the public-address system. They posted notices near every employee entrance, and the Memorandum and Correspondence Distribution Center shipped leaflets to every location within the district, stating:

THOSE WHO ARE NOT VOLUNTARILY VACCINATED WILL BE EXCUSED FROM THEIR VOCATION 90 DAYS FROM THIS DAY.

They posted a notice at the warehouse where we stored our work vehicles as well. In fact, that's how we learned of the policy and the silent transition from contractor to our falling into the employ of the hospital. The acquisition was made—or announced, at least—the first week of October, and we were given until the last week of December to adhere. Vaccination booths popped up in the lobbies of nearly every facility, clinic, and satellite along our routes, even the warehouses. Because of that, most complied within the week. Still, they sent reminders and updated lists of tardy individuals at each week's end right up until the Christmas holiday.

Did they hound the hospital workers?

Whenever one went in for medical treatment, urgent or otherwise, they would be refused care if they weren't yet vaccinated. Even if they were bringing one of their children in for medical treatment, all family members must become vaccinated.

What about the Carriers?

Most jumped at the opportunity for free vaccines. But, one did quit outright on the very first day of notification. Right then and there. He simply turned and went home without saying a word to anyone. Another protested. He felt the vaccinations were part of a ploy. He even got another Carrier to join him in his protest.

Ploy?

One of paranoid proportions. In his desperation, he started a petition. He hoped to gain my signature after learning I was yet to receive my vaccine. He asked whether I'd got my shot, and I told him *no*. He didn't ask why or whether I intended to, rather he launched into what sounded like something he'd rehearsed at home.

Soapboxing?

Yes, in a way, that's a way to put it. But, to me, it sounded like more of a calculated rant.

How so?

The words in his little speech were above what he used in normal conversation, his cadence had a stutter to it which underpinned how he questioned if the words he used were the right ones and if they truly meant what he thought they meant, only that he'd heard them used by someone else—and whomever it was sounded smart enough to convince him of the plot.

You make this guy sound like a parrot, a Mockingbird.

That's another way to say it, yes. But given the way he looked it was more like a giant turkey vulture with his shiny beet red bald head. I was always waiting for him to fall over clutching his chest.

Was he a nonessential?

Those—that was something people were not called quite yet. Not at that time. That time came way after. No, he was weird though.

Weird?

Yeah, odd. When this thing with the voluntary vaccinations came about, he got real weird, real fast. He stood a head taller than me, see. That first morning the notice was posted, he shadowed me every step of the way while I started my day, checking my vehicle, readying it to travel, loading up the coolers, booting up my scanner. He cut me off every time I tried to check off another box.

He stalked you around the warehouse hoping it would convince you to side with him, sign his petition?

Bingo.

What language is that?

It means you guessed right. Dammit. You've never played bingo?

Bingo.

Your loss. I listened to the reasons this guy listed for not getting the shots out of pure politeness. Yes, he had a list. But I also listened out of my own desperate need for amusement. Not to mention, he never paused once to take a breath or give me a moment to argue or interject my own opinions on the matter, or even agree with him—had I been inclined to do so. It seemed obvious he didn't want to be interrupted. He wanted to be heard though, that's for certain. And the look that crept onto his face when he finished a thought was enough to make you think he was surprised by the things he said.

He surprised his own self, you mean?

I do, and the reasons he gave were plenteous, to say the very least. And passionate.

Sounds so.

What I can still recall across the years are what were most likely the most outlandish. Some had a bit of logic behind them, yes, though I couldn't possibly recite them all now. But the illogical, the illogical were bred from the fear-mongering news pundits he listened to while he drove.

Broadcast radio?

Yeah, before it became public address only. See, he was certain the vaccines were going to make him ill. So sick, he'd have to go to his doctor for further treatment and pay them money to treat the illness they created in him. He'd also heard of the possibility of nanobots being injected along with the vaccines, so they can track us, he said. He thought the nanobots could listen to you and they could kill you with them if they wanted. Clog an artery or something, he said. He told me about this fear he had that some of the inactive ingredients in the serums could cause mental diseases or a breakdown of brain chemistry, shorting out synapses or an all-out rewiring of one's brain chemistry. He was one of those who believed all of the above. Every last word.

So you got the shot?

I tried.

Tried? You found difficulty, or excuses?

Reasons, not excuses. Each time I arrived at a stop along my route there was a line waiting to receive their vaccine. I even tried to circumvent the line, but it was to no avail.

Even early in the morning?

Yes, even early in the morning. First thing. In fact, I was the one who delivered the cases of the vaccines to the places along my route.

You did?

I did. Every Tuesday and Thursday. Hundreds upon hundreds of vials of the vaccine over those three months. I'd ask at the nurse's station when they signed for the coolers, but their answers were always the same: first come, first served.

Isn't that a little ironic? You bringing the vaccines to the nurses yet you weren't there early enough to be the first in line.

It pissed me off to no end. I even left the Memorandum and Correspondence Distribution Center before the vaccines were brought down once or twice. Not out of spite, not completely. That's just how busy my days got. I couldn't wait around for any reason. If I did, I'd be late to my next stop and the next stop, and the stop after that. Tardiness in this job works like falling dominoes—always keep that in mind. Despite how full my days were, or are, I did try to get vaccinated a few times before I was notified I had to go in to see—someone. Human Resources, I think. Then security. I thought I was to be officially warned or fired—figured security would take my access badge and escort me out of the building.

That wasn't the case, obviously.

We were left to figure out a lot of things for ourselves during the transition. Notes and notices, memorandums, policies and such, appeared in our mailboxes from time to time. Someone scrawled updates on the message board, but our manager disappeared. Fired. Transferred. Something. His office sat emptied. Computer, desk, chairs, calendar. Everything. He was just gone one day. He worked from home so often no one really knew when it was we began working without a net.

A net? What were the nets used for?

It's—ah—fuck. Just another dead metaphor.

It's a what? Never mind. What did you find out when you went to see whoever it was you went to see?

Short version? I didn't have to get the shot after all.

HOME SWEET HOME

Again, why don't you just go home, watch some programing, read some of those books? The ones older than me you're so partial to.

Home?

Yeah, home.

They've got me up in the towers like everyone else.

Uh-huh. Are you telling me you don't keep a place out in the fringes?

No, I've an assigned dwelling within the towers like everyone else.

And?

And a house can be made a home. The towers, they cannot.

They can't?

No. They're nothing but vertical corrals for the masses.

Corral? Wouldn't that essentially make you the Judas cow?

Essentially?

Yeah. Well, home is where the heart is, right? My grandmother had that embroidered and framed in her first tower dwelling.

Did that hang to the left or the right of blond Jesus?

Meaning?

Meaning they're both bullshit, meant to comfort the masses. They're only real purpose is to give the nice people warm fuzzies.

Is there something wrong with comforted citizens?

Why're you shaking your head? I say with a laugh. Was hers a warm place round about Christmastime?

Yeah. Of course. Why?

And her home before that?

You're asking if they froze her out, aren't ya?

Were you around then? Old enough to remember?

Remember what?

The beginning of Burr's second term.

Second? You're still counting then?

Somewhat, you could say. It's easier to keep track of than A.D..

After Death?

After Democracy.

After? We—we still vote, he says nodding his head and raising his eyebrows as if to pause the conversation for me to come back into the here and now.

Oh, you don't participate?

We all must participate. You know that, don't you? There is no more voluntary polling. It's requisite of every citizen. As long as you're literate enough to fill out the forms and not mislead *them* in terms of your blood quantums.

How do you vote if you're never home? How do the census workers track you down for you to even cast a vote?

You think you can hide from *them*?

You seem like a guy who's partial to his privacy.

Privacy? How the hell did that ever become a part of your vocabulary? Privacy died long before you were born.

You ever wonder if you might be a bit—ah—a bit paranoid?

Hmm, I see. You're measuring your words now?

I'm not as well read as you.

As far as me being paranoid, I would say not that at all. Not one bit. Complacency will show you the way to the grave quicker than anything in this world. Paranoia is fine, it keeps you alert, keeps your head on a swivel. I wouldn't worry about paranoia unless I started to see things that weren't there. And I do see the census takers. And I do vote. But, if you're like me, you think of it more in terms of them polling the people in order to see who supports the executive administration and its policies. To make sure you're still rooting for the home team.

You don't think there's a real elected governance anymore? Why not? What brought you to that conclusion?

Governance? I'm guessing you did not learn that word from a medical pamphlet.

No, I did not.

There was no one thing that you can point a finger to, but Burr's second term is when the policies began. Or were ended, I guess you could say.

Ended?

Well, when he set out to cease what President Geneva Puryear set into motion.

What do you mean? What has he put a stop to?

See, this is all you've ever known. This is the only world you can conceive of because you were conceived in this world.

Yes, I was born naturally. But you already knew that. Why bother mentioning it?

Perspective.

Any chance you were born naturally?

I was—in a way.

In a way?

I was a twin.

Oh. I see. Is that how you do it? The two of you switch off and *they* think you're running the roads day and night? Tricky. Twins don't make it anymore.

No, they do not. Not since *they* walled off the NICU, made it look like it was never there in the first place. But twins didn't always make it home back when I was born either.

Excuse me?

My twin. My older brother.

Yeah, what about him?

He was stillborn.

He's still what?

Short version? He was unable to take a breath on his own.

And they wouldn't assist way back then either?

He'd been without air for too long by the time they could do anything.

Wow. Sorry. That's ah—

Yeah. It is.

So, you weren't born into an age of medical miracles either?

No, that came way after me. After my children even.

And ended before I came around.

A good many things ended, yes, but Burr left it up to the districts by putting an end to what you think of as entitlements. He gave governors and mayors and commissioners and councils the permission to say no. Or, no more. People were given choices on the local level.

Choices?

Yeah, that's where the districts were dreamt up for the most part. Some argued that they were ultimatums. Others went along thinking the next one to come along would undue things, right Burr's wrongs and such.

Are you still waiting?

Holding one's breath isn't ever advisable.

Neither is shivering to death.

Oh, so they did freeze Grandma out.

You guessed it.

She accepted an assigned dwelling in the towers then?

She did.

Was it to her liking?

She was accepting of it, said it was comparable to her home atop the piedmont.

I laugh, *The piedmont.* She lives high in the towers then?

She did. She's since transitioned. And what's comical about that?

The council wasn't too original in the naming of the district's divisions: Lakeside, East Hillside, Central Hillside, Piedmont, the Zenith Sea. Well, West does smack of some originality being it is actually south on the compass. We've covered this though, haven't we?

We have, but hasn't West been abandoned?

Shit no, there's still a satellite out there.

It's the fringes though.

Oh, well, shit. Good to know. I should turn us back around then, huh?

What?

Just because there're no towers there doesn't mean it's part of the fringes.

What does it mean?

It means if you cross over into the West you better belong there.

It's not part of the Makwa forest?

It hasn't been taken back yet.

The hunters do have it then?

They do, for now.

And you've no problem with the hunters?

And they've no problem with me.

No?

Nope. Not at all. My grandmother's house still stands in the shadows of the hunter's hall.

Wasn't it lost in the fires?

No, and the makwa haven't made it a den.

Not yet.

No, not yet.

The dogs?

What, do you want to see if they are domestic in the least, take a pup from the pack?

Dogs aren't allowed in the towers.

That is where the packs came from.

Huh? The mayingan?

They're dogs, they're not mayingan.

They're what happened when the dogs were abandoned by their owners when everyone resettled in the towers. They were allowed to fuck freely. Free from intelligent design.

You know this how?

Watched it happen.

What, you pull up a chair and sat there with a bowl of popcorn?

No, but I've sat behind this wheel and ran these roads long enough to watch the spayed and neutered dogs die off. I've seen the chihuahuas and yorkies and pugs hunted down by the bigger dogs as well as the makwa and the mayingan. That's some heartbreaking shit to see. Mutual of Omaha, if you know what I mean.

I don't. Not in the least.

Yeah, well, it used to be a nature show they'd air on the Public Broadcasting System when I was a kid. They showed nature at its most majestic, and violent. Looking back now, I think the best part was watching it with my family and hearing my grandma cry out to the television—completely beside herself, shaking, power-dragging her cigarettes—asking why the cameraman would not stop what he was doing and help the poor defenseless prey out of their sad, desperate situations.

I've still no clue. The dogs, they don't look like the mayingan?

No, not altogether. I saw the shepherds breed with the labradors and their fur darkened, then blackened. The spaniels bred in with the herding dogs and their fur thickened. All of them began to run in packs together. Sizeable packs. Bigger and bigger as time progressed. Their ears pricked, and their tails curled. The dogs that were part shepherd, lab, spaniel, and herding dogs, mixed in with the ones that were once mastiffs, and those pups came across packs of pit bulls that'd mixed in with the sled dogs.

Fuck.

All that took about three years' time. That's about when they stopped looking to people for food and started looking at people as food.

Fuck.

Basically.

Did *they* freeze you out of your home, too?

No, there was a time when I'd pay for my utilities six months in advance and not stress about missing a meal or having to scrape on by until my next check came in.

You're paid that well to do this?

Oh, no. Things didn't cost as much as they let on now. Plus, I rented a place that was warmed by steam in the winter.

What a waste.

Waste?

Of water.

Oh, no. Then the lake nearly came up to the central boulevard.

W-what? Ha-ha, okay then.

Why're you laughing about that?

The canyon, you mean?

The canyon that sits at the southernmost edge

of the district was a harbor and the Bay of Saint Louis back then.

Oh?

Why else would the bridges raise to an arch over the canyon?

Good question. But you're asking the wrong person, I am not an engineer.

Are you an imbecile?

Are you an asshole?

Inquiring minds want to know, but when my bills came in the mail way back then, back when the district wastefully—as you said—warmed my home with water, I checked the box and added a little extra to the amount I paid so others who warmed their homes with electricity wouldn't freeze come the colder months.

Did many others do the same?

I believe so.

So why did my grandmother damn near freeze to death then?

The box disappeared.

What?

The shared heat program got repealed. No announcement was made. The little empty square in the upper right-hand corner of the bill just went away one month and it was never an option after that. No one could contribute to the collective charity after that.

And after that?

After that, *they* lifted the law saying your

utilities could not be shut off until the spring if you became delinquent with the payment. *They* being the Duluth District council.

That's shitty.

Shitty is not people going to check on family after their lights went dark to find mom, dad, and the kids—curled up together in one bed—everyone covered in a thick coat of frost.

They did that?

They did if the bill collectors didn't come knocking in time. And if you couldn't afford to heat your home or keep the lights turned on, it became kind of like when you needed a lawyer yet couldn't quite afford one.

Meaning?

Meaning one was appointed for you.

A home?

A dwelling.

In the cluster of towers *they* built in the Central Hillside?

And Bingo was his name, oh.

And those towers were nice and toasty for all the grandmas, weren't they?

It's a safe bet.

Did they pay to warm all those people?

Didn't have to.

What?

The towers were brand new.

Yeah?

They're built of solid concrete.

And?

Cement.

Yeah?

You need to read a little more widely. Cement goes through a chemical reaction and takes years to harden all the way.

Do what now?

Shit. That chemical reaction gives off heat. It radiates its own heat, see. They didn't have to flip a switch and warm the coils for years. If your dwelling was internal, you'd swear they were trying to cook you sometimes.

Core temp.

Correct.

But aren't all buildings heated with geothermal energy now?

Correct. At least that's what I've heard.

Flipped a switch?

Okay, there was no switch for them to flip then, huh? *They* turned a valve then, didn't *they*? I stand corrected. Congratulations.

Hey, sorry, I'm just making conversation here. Didn't mean to exude sarcasm.

You're accustomed to walking into a place and the lights flicker to life, don't get how flipping a switch is something of an expression.

A dead metaphor, you mean?

See the trestle?

Trestle? The bridge up there?

We're here.

Here?

Well, I wasn't going to outright assume, but I suppose you've never seen the place. You did say how you thought it was all abandoned, didn't you?

Abandoned?

Yeah, abandoned. You saying so leads me to dare speculate you've never seen the place.

This is The West?

That it is.

Is that a clock tower climbing out of the canopy of the makwa forest?

Your eyes do not deceive.

That's Hunter Hall I'm looking at, is that what you are telling me?

Whatever they've taken to calling it, yes.

How few are the hunters now?

I can't quite tell whether he's asking a question or making a statement. But I do know he doesn't quite get what he's looking at, or who the hunters are. He's thinking they're some sort of maddened freedom fighters who live just outside the fringes of the district, or cannibals, like the rumors say. He has no earthly idea what he's laying his eyes on. Or that if he can see the tower, they can see the both of us. Even this far out. He won't be able to grasp how there's an expanse of buildings sprawled for a square kilometer beneath the branches, but there aren't any other than the clocktower that climbs higher than the trees. He can't quite comprehend people living any other way than being stacked on top of one another in the honeycomb arrangement of the towers. He'd never be able to wrap his head around the high school's Olympic-sized pool being turned into a terrarium, a greenhouse capable of feeding the five-hundred hunters holed up inside season after season—years upon years—after *they* repealed the right-to-farm laws, putting an end to anyone attempting to feed their family free of whatever they sprayed onto our food that killed the slugs and the mosquitos and the biting flies and the boll weevils and the bees as well as anyone who couldn't stomach the cocktail of herbicides and pesticides and enriched fertilizers *they* said were better than the black dirt that'd stain my grandmother's moccasins when she toiled with her rose bushes each and every spring, back when everything grew so naturally and so quickly that the next-door neighbor was outside each and every day clipping his grass back down just as soon as the morning sunlight evaporated the last of the morning dew.

Are we getting out here, Jon?

No.

You're getting out here?

Yes, that is what it looks like. Your eyes do not deceive you.

What am I doing?

Little as possible.

What?

You can get behind the engine block if it makes you feel safer.

If?

If. I said. Just don't argue. Do it.

NEW LEGISLATION ELIMINATES NATIONAL PUBLIC LANDS ACROSS NORTH AMERICAN TERRITORIES

By Graeme Barrentine
October 1, 2041

DENVER — Senator Mayer Schwent said districts will be able to sell public lands in what he dubs a revision and clarification of the overly antiquated 'Homestead Act' on July 29, days before the August recess began. Senator Schwent outlined three bills concerning North American public lands in front of an emphatic crowd at the National Agricultural Institute. He spoke against the existence of nationally-managed public lands, which he asserted will soon be open for development and managed by individual districts, eliminating the need for yet another national oversight agency.

These three bills oppose the existing sentiment of keeping public lands free of development and available for public use by North American citizens and foreign visitors alike. Senator Schwent rallied support saying, "Our agricultural lands are in crisis. A second dust bowl is on the horizon. Playtime is over."

Schwent has been reported to be on President Geoff Burr's short list to serve as Chief of Staff to replace Cloyce Scheer, who resigned last month. Burr said he will decide on his replacement within the week.

Schwent outlined three points of his new Homestead Act to the crowd during his speech. Ultimately, his proposals will hand national lands over to their custodial districts and allow for development. Bidding on public lands should be settled before the next spring months.

Schwent's first proposal abolishes national lands designated as National Monuments by President Theodore Roosevelt's American Antiquities Act of 1906. With what Schwent calls the "North American Rural Communities Protection Act," citizens will be entrusted with what he says, "should be their land to do with as their district's needs dictate."

The North American Rural Communities Protection Act will prohibit any future president from designating any future national monuments without first receiving a unanimous collective chain of approval from the senate, house, and custodial district.

Senator Mayer Schwent's second bill will pave a path for the building of housing on formally national lands, courtesy of the introduction of this "new" Homestead Act. Essentially giving districts the power to sell or lease public lands to help alleviate their district's housing shortages.

The Homestead Act of 1866

relinquished 270 million acres of land from national possession, allowing private ownership, which made way for the westward expansion. Schwent has hailed the act as one of the nation's great accomplishments alongside the Medicine Lodge Treaty of October 1867 which relocated the Indigenous peoples away from European-American settlements, making 60,000 square miles habitable for colonial immigrants.

"My revised Homestead Act expands the law to allow petitions for land use which will best benefit the citizens of the concerned districts," Schwent said.

The senator's third bill will transfer national lands under district control, a goal he fears will take years to complete as populaces shift and per capita quotas are argued and appealed.

"It is only when the districts control their own lands that citizens will truly see progress in these deficient times," Schwent said.

The National Agricultural Institute, a national food and health policy think tank headquartered in the district of Atlanta, served as the launch point for Schwent's agenda outlining the abolishment of national public lands.

Schwent said his goals are "a huge task — nothing that anyone before has attempted to accomplish."

He concluded — and contradicted — his address by citing several other precedents of public land transfers, which went entirely ignored by his audience.

In 2029, Atlanta District Gov. William Wyler published an open letter urging Burr to rescind the protection of national monuments standing on fertile lands. Wyler's letter became the springboard behind the legislation that significantly reduced the size of both Effigy Mounds National Monument and Tallgrass Prairie National Preserve. This too triggered a backlash from the outdoor industry leaders including their Outdoor Retailer convention being pulled out of Atlanta in protest, moving the gathering to Denver.

Schwent told the crowd at the National Agricultural Institute that the "upper-crust elite" intend to transform the North American West into, "pretty little tourist towns filled with uninhabited vistas while the good people of this nation starve. They like to say how the national lands are an inheritance for everyone born in North America to experience. But the benefits they dole out seem to only flow one way — their way." Schwent continued to say, "They get their playgrounds in Moab and Aspen and Mont Tremblant and the Adirondacks while the rest of us are poisoned day after day from the meals we are forced to eat from boxes and plastic pouches shipped from processing plants across the oceans."

Schwent hopes for his speech to gain traction across the districts, ignite conversation, local legislation, and bring about great change.

ZOMBI

Jonathan, my sweet. You're forty.

Almost. No need to round up, now is there, my dear?

How do you not get it? *They're* using you the same as the generals and the admirals did for all those years, honey. *They* used you in the wars and *they're* using you now. It's predatory. It's pathetic that you don't see it.

Oh, I'm pathetic? Is that so? I'm getting promoted. I'm not the one getting removed from my vocation at the hospital. Am I, *Doctor*?

Oh, that's great. Have you ever considered that they're only promoting you because you never take sick days and they don't have to give you medical benefits because the government has to foot that bill until you drop dead?

I'm being promoted because I do the job, well. I'm never late, I've never lost a specimen, I've never damaged a vehicle. Shit, I finish my route forty-five minutes to an hour faster than the guy

152

who trained me. Did you know that? I never get sick because I use the antiseptic foam before I go into each laboratory and immediately after I leave. I'm careful. I know how diseases are transmitted. I don't touch the door handles. I use my foot to push the doors open or my elbow to turn the latches.

Jesus, Jonathan. That shit weakens your immunity when you use it as much as you do.

It's policy. There are cameras everywhere in that place.

It doesn't do what you think it does. Besides, who's going to write you up? When was the last time you saw that boss of yours?

Thanks for the advice, *Doctor*, but whenever someone initials my scanner without taking off their nasty-ass gloves first, I wipe the whole thing down with that foam. It is the same with the Grimace-looking one who always used to wear the purple scrubs, who won't stop coughing into her hands and always wants to sign because she thinks she is in charge.

Don't do that *Doctor* shit. I'm your wife dammit. Do you know how you sound when you say it? It's condescending. I don't need that when I come home.

Okay, sorry, I didn't mean it to come off like that. But you're sick all the damn time. I'm not sick. Fucking ever.

You carry that shit on you. You drive all around

town to all the satellites all day long, then come home to me and get me sick.

Don't you work with kids all day long?

Broken kids. Not sick kids.

Out of the dozens of kids you see during the day, none are sick?

That's not it, don't you see, sweetie. But you know what? If any kids do come in looking sick, they are made to wear a mask by reception or go home, reschedule. We take it seriously with the kids we see.

Your point?

The point is the stuff people are being screened for at the satellites is viral, most of it airborne, you don't have to touch anything. The stuff hangs in the air and gets on you and when you come through that door and hug me and give me a kiss, I get it. I get sick with that stuff. Then you see me getting sick and sit on the opposite end of the couch and act like I'm going to get you sick. But it's you who makes me suffer and it's me who's going to be eliminated at the hospital.

How's it my fault? I didn't deem physical rehabilitation nonessential treatment.

Fault? Fault, no, you're a fucking medical wonder. I wish I had your problems. Shit, if they could, they'd probably bottle your problem and sell it. But you're probably good for business.

What?

You.

Yeah? What about me?

You—walking around—getting patients sicker than what they were when they came in to see their doctors when their aim was to figure out what ailment they were suffering. Then, in walks Jonathan, teeming with god-knows-what. But, the donors get treated for whatever brought them in in the first place—meanwhile—whatever you exposed them to incubates and goes untreated, so they go back and get seen and get tested for that and probably run into you again.

You think you've stumbled onto some sort of epiphany, or something? Everyone knows a hospital is anything but a sterile environment. Isn't there some disease you can only get by going to a hospital? MRSA, right? Isn't that what it's called?

Christ, you're like a goddamned zombi shuffling around town wrapped in a smallpox blanket.

What do you want me to do about it? Shall we turn the mudroom into a delousing booth, dear? Should I strip in the backyard and burn my clothes before I come inside? What? Tell me what you want me to do?

I want you to sleep in the basement.

Fuck—you—Doctor.

What?

You heard me. Why don't you sleep down there?

It's damp down there, cold.

Yeah, it'll probably soothe your fever.

Me? You're the one sweating your ass off. It's sixty-seven degrees in here. Look at the thermostat.

I have a physical job; this uniform doesn't breathe.

No. No. No, you've got something again. Keep away from me.

Yeah, I'll keep away from you all right.

THE HUNTER

The West wasn't always this way then?

I fill my lungs with air, wonder how to word this so he'll get it. He presses me, asks again with a *Hmm?*

No. That, it was not.

Who the hell lived way out here then?

The workers.

The workers?

Yes. Blue collar workers. Ever heard that term?

Can't say I have.

Well the workers lived out here while the owners lived in the east—Lakeside—and the Woodlands, the town of Herman, too.

They were made to live out here then?

No, they just couldn't afford to live anywhere else is all.

I see. How did the workers become the hunters then?

Necessity, I say. And leave it at that.

Necessity?

That's what I said. Surely you aren't of the mind that swinging a golf club could somehow ready one for a society unraveled.

Well, no.

No is right. The workers rolled with the punches while the privileged learned their lives were superficial. It's why they're the first to fling themselves out an office window when their plummeted trade value whittles their existence down to only what they can hold in their hands. They don't own anything, they've never built anything they can call their own. Their lives are leased, mortgaged, borrowed. It's a paper existence. They don't know what it means to live within their means. They've never watched coins kept in a jar dwindle down to nothing. Their life ebbs and flows with the successes and failings of financial dice-rolling. But they're a forgetful bunch, see, while we workers remember—a plague of generational remembrance. The owners thought they would always have the upper hand in this world, generation after generation.

It seems an unfortunate thing for them to assume.

Yeah? Fuck em. They didn't bat an eye when they began the labeling of people.

So there was mislabeling?

No, that's the wrong way to look at it. The labeling was the misstep, see. Generalizing any group of people is never the proper course. Neither is grouping folks.

Is that so?

No, it'll never be the right way to go about things. You ever try to stomp on an ant so hard your knee feels as though it could burst, and when you move your foot said ant carries on unaffected?

I couldn't say the last time I saw one, but, yes, I get where you're headed.

It's the same when you label one a nonessential. Or the wrong ones, more appropriately.

So what are you, when in the West, if you are not a hunter?

Prey.

You're paid enough to be prey?

They feed and house me. I do as I am asked, and I want for naught.

Asked? Told, you mean?

Yeah, no. Asked. And who told you I am not a hunter?

Come again.

Born here, raised here. I'll never shake the stink. No one ever does.

How're you living among the essentials then?

I wasn't educated with the hunters. I left before then. I was educated with those from the woodlands and the lakeside.

How?

My grandparents were buried in the Oneota hills before my secondary education began.

The Oneota hills? That's part of the Makwa forest, right?

Yes, now they are.

And back then?

Manicured, serene even. A place of calm and solace. It overlooked the streets that made up the neighborhoods where the deceased once resided.

Live here, die here.

A point of pride for many. But those who live around here can't be buried there.

No? Why not?

Have to be dead first, I laugh.

What? He asks, even more confused, adding a chuckle of his own after finally getting the joke. Do you ever go visit your grandparents?

It's overgrown forest, not even part of the fringes.

How hard could it be to navigate?

The place is a hundred acres.

A hundred acres of woods?

Yes, that's right. It's a hundred acres of woods surrounded by more woods, and I am no Christopher Robin.

What? Who?

Don't worry about it, but he does like those silly ol bears.

He *likes* the makwa? He's feral, I take it?

Sure.

These are strange times. People cope differently.

Different strokes, different folks.

So, a hunter?

By birth.

Oh, if *they* only knew.

You plan on telling *them*?

They won't hear a peep from me.

Not that it matters much, *they* decide what you are, what *they* need you to be.

They decided you'd be a carrier?

That's what they needed from me. Need. I'll continue this for a good long while.

You are grizzled if nothing else.

Why, thank you.

The two of us may have a different understanding of that word.

Or a different understanding of what is needed in this world. That would be the great plague of this generation.

What's that?

Want versus need, self over other, so on and so forth. We are social animals. Were—social animals. Pack animals. But animals first and foremost.

What are you meaning?

See, there was a time when neighborhoods were busy with dogs. Dogs're pack animals as well yet made to live in solitude for the most part, as pets. I'm talking some ways back here.

All right.

They had jobs to do.

Companions?

No, the jobs they were hardwired for.

Protection.

In a way—but more than that—a sort of early warning system for their masters. Are you following now?

I'm listening.

Keep listening.

If one of these dogs would hear something they didn't like or thought sounded suspicious, they'd sound the alarm.

Bark?

Bark, howl, snarl, growl, yelp, yap depending on the breed and disposition. But they would not be ignored until their masters took note. The neighborhood would erupt in sound, become an unignorable cacophony. Lights would flicker on, some right away while others would wait and act as though it'd go away if they just ignored it long enough. But for the most part, people would come and see what was the matter. Sometimes it was someone who didn't belong, other times it could be leaves tumbling down the street. Or a tomcat.

I see.

It didn't matter whether your dog got along with the other neighborhood dogs, they became embroiled, got into a crowd mentality, to do what they could to put an end to the intrusion. Some would work to jump their fences or burrow beneath them in order to handle it outright. Even if it was merely rustling leaves.

Rustling leaves?

Well, when you can't see what all is happening, you trust others that things aren't as they should be, understand?

Social animals.

Indeed. Like us, once upon a time. But when something we hear becomes equivocated, say, like, social programs, some people stop barking after so long because it becomes confusing. They're not sure whether it's worth barking over any longer, and those who won't shut up about them are simply seen as neurotic—or so *they'd* like us to think.

They are the intrusion in this story?

Don't get ahead of me. Those social programs were something we heard talked about so often and a term applied to so many different things, we started to forget what exactly they were. But whatever they were, they were nothing if not a drain. That point was talked about more than anything else on the matter. The drain, that is.

So, you pull the plug on them, get rid of them and let the drain become less of a drain. In theory, at least.

In theory?

That's the way it was framed by those trusted to deal with such things.

Burr, you mean?

To begin with.

But he had no knowledge of drains.

You saying he wasn't a plumber?

No more than he was a politician. He couldn't define a social program. He only knew his opponents promoted them and wanted to expand them.

And he began to cut them?

He did. Some without notice. And he villainized their champion. But some programs people just don't stop to wonder whether they're social programs. They're more like givens.

Entitlements?

Precisely. Part of living life in a democracy. People thought these programs were for those who couldn't take care of themselves and those uninformed people grew tired of helping others who seemed to be doing nothing for themselves.

It's reasonable.

Sure, that could be argued. But there are avenues in life which everyone will invariably need help with.

If you say so.

That said, there were programs people never need, never use in their entire lifetimes. If they're lucky.

Sounds like a drain.

To the individual, yes.

Well, if everyone took care of themselves, they wouldn't need to worry about the group because the group would be taken care of, right? A group of individuals taking care of themselves.

Right, until your home catches fire and you call

for help and listen to the message telling you how the number for the emergency services has been disconnected. No one is answering that call. So, you have to take care of it yourself, right? and all the while you're trying to remember the last time you saw a fire truck barreling down the street to help some poor soul in need.

But it's a fire.

It was a socially funded program. Was, I say, drumming my thumbs on the steering wheel. It was a drain. The old eyesores burned up, one after the other. Sometimes an entire neighborhood would go up in a single evening. The flames would flicker and jump from one house to the next, the way girls would play hopscotch down the sidewalk while clueless little schoolboys watched from afar, unsure as to what was going on. Old wiring wore out, shorted out. Poof, I tell him, exploding my fingers out from my balled-up fist.

That makes no sense, what about the police?

The police?

Yes, the police.

Oh, you're mistaken. We are policed, yes, but not by *the* police.

Who then?

Here? Here the hunters are something of a neighborhood watch.

Have you ever hunted, had to hunt? However you say it?

I was a soldier.

And you've hunted humans?

I did as *they* asked. I too was part of a special security detail.

What was this special security detail asked to do?

On paper?

Sure.

We went places where no one else was sent to extract people who shouldn't have taken it upon themselves to visit in the first place. No way, no how. Morons on a mission from god.

You sound perturbed with these people.

I saw no reason to retrieve them.

No?

No. If god be with them, who could be against them? That's the saying, right?

Certainly.

Well, they learned it wasn't quite so rhetorical a thing to ask. A question they should have never begged. They found out just how weighty their god's word is once they ventured outside their congregations and into areas of active conflict, especially when the locals bowed their heads in prayer a bit differently.

And you got them out how?

However. There was a myriad of resources in our toolbox, and the evangelicals who governed us spared no expense to bring them home.

Evangelicals?

Well, purportedly.

Purportedly?

Those with the desire to conserve what made America great, backed by those who made the tools of our trade. Those who ultimately made the decisions for us to use our skill sets in ways which would preserve humanity.

Your voice doesn't smack of warm remembrance.

No?

No. Though the plot thickens.

The nation which forgets its defenders will itself be forgotten.

Is that so?

It's a warning which has been echoed for close to two thousand years.

And you feel forgotten?

Me? We, you mean.

They—who know all—forgot you, both a hunter and a defender?

I am simply a driver. I carry things to and fro, back and forth, point A to point B.

A simple man.

Indeed.

The program that saw after us—those of us who made it back as much as we were sent away—was too socially funded, and one day ceased to exist.

They did that?

We saw it coming. We were trained to do without. Sleep wherever. Bivouac under the stars, or bridges. Eat what we could, no matter the taste or lack thereof. Adapt to what presented itself to us, overcome the next obstacle, improvise what we must to do what is needed. We were the test group for all this, I say pointing to everything and nothing with one hand while lowering the blades of the plow with the other, anchoring the vehicle to the ground in doing so.

A gas mask?

The air is noxious here. Chemicals from the abandoned paper mill, fumes from the waste treatment facility from back when the water receded and seized the pipes and processes, topsoil turned into a cloud that never reaches the sky.

And mouse ears?

Who's the leader of the pack that's made for you and me?

Leader?

CAT & MOUSE

Shaddox, that you?
　Yeah.

　Sergeant Shaddox?
　Yup, the prodigal son returns. Motherfucker dresses like a mouse, walks like a cat.
　What do you expect, aye? Everyone's losing their minds these days.
　You ain't lying.

　I'm unarmed.
　Hey, like hell you are.

　Lower your weapons for fuck's sake.

　Are you done? Go ahead and shove that wand up your ass, why don't you?
　Hey, I got something, he announces to the overwatch, ignoring the thing I said. That's good. I'm glad to see them doing their jobs regardless of

who they're dealing with. But still, I roll my eyes at all the pomp and circumstance. Not that anyone could see.

What? I ask. You want me to take off my belt? Beat your ass while I'm at it?

Calm down, Jonathan.
Hey there, niiji.

Let him in.

Open up.

Don't shoot the messenger, young buck.

Who's this sergeant?
Yeah, was, he's a sleeper, resettled into the circumcenter. Served in the desert wars.
Oh yeah? Well, lah-di-dah. Which front?
All.
What do you mean by that?
Fucking—all of them. That's what I mean. Spent so much time in the sun he lost half an ear to skin ah—what do you call it—cancer.
Shit looks nasty. How the hell is he not locked up in some padded room?
Now, what fun would that be? You think they want the nutty ones who know how to do some damage locked away from the rest of the world? Who the hell else would there be to kick off a

proper thinning of the herd if they started endorsing that shit? You've got to have an ace in the hole, don'tcha know?

Shh...zip it now. Watch him close. Don't be afraid to drop him if you have to.

You can take off the mask in here. We're all bathed.
You trying to offend us, Shaddox?
Don't remember you offending quite so easily. These kids softening you up?

Looks like someone sewed some buttons onto some shoe leather, like Caroline.
Fuck off. I'm old, not deaf. And it's Coraline, dumb fuck.
Shoe leather doesn't sweat like that.
Hey! You better not be bringing that shit that's thinning out the towers in here.
You serious with that shit? Who the fuck—

To what do we owe this pleasure?
Owe? I need a reason to come see my cousin?

We're all related. Ain't that what you always say? You coming here less and less makes us more and more suspicious, Shaddox. Why don't you just tell us why you decided to traipse through the trees and knock on our door.

Well, fuck me. What have you been reading? Finally find the library, did ya?

Talk, Jon.

Well, speak of the devil. Cousin, I got somebody new in my truck, asking lots of questions—more than he needs to. You know what I'm getting at?

And you're one to criticize a guy for being chatty? Pot calling the kettle black, aye? I don't remember being able to get a word in while you were around back when we were kids, unless Grandma gave you a book to read.

That ain't it. Figured I'd clean out my truck before he figured what all I transport.

What? When did shit, piss, and blood, become some state secret? You afraid it'll ruin the romance and no one else will sign up to be a runner?

Afraid he'll notice the Lakeside satellite sent back a box of inoculations no one seems to have asked for and can't be reshelved. Seems it's paid for, so it's disappeared from the system. Barcodes have already dissolved.

Shelf life?

It's sealed in dry ice. It'll take about twelve hours to get the bottles out once the seal is broken, then it'll start to weaken, lose potency.

It's not that placebo shit? Or are you bringing us that blue-light-special serum they sell at the child development centers but still tell people it's the same vaccines they're getting on the top floors of the towers?

No, it's not, and, no, I'm not. Look, can we talk someplace else without these little shits interjecting all the damn time? It's for those who pay into the system, not for those who work for remittance. Lakeside, like I said.

He shakes his head telling me no, we have to stay put, and asks, It's for the current strain?

This strain, yah, before it mutates.

Before someone from the circumcenter strolls in here, you mean—exposing us to some new shit no one's worked out a cure for yet.

Come again?

Nothing.

You know full-fucking-well I'm immune.

The sweat pouring off your head along with that patchy beard of yours don't make you look much like a picture of health. Not to mention the ear.

What ear?

Exactly.

And it's not patchy. There's white and gray mixed in amongst the black.

Not from back here, it ain't. I just see you looking mangey.

You don't remember what they taught us then?

About what?

Migizi.

Might as well be a mythical creature, Cousin. Nothing round here but wakes of vultures.

You're telling me that you don't remember what they told us? About it taking seven years for their heads to turn white?

Yeah, so?

So, that's how you become an elder.

How's that again?

One white hair at a time.

That's a cute little notion, Jonathan. What do you want for your troubles?

Food.

Are they not feeding you in the towers?

I'd like something that doesn't say MADE IN on the side of the pouch. I'd like something that doesn't come in a pouch, for that matter.

Oh, and you're asking me if I've softened. You call yourself a soldier wanting something other than what the government decides you need.

Hey, if the soldiers are eating salads nowadays, shouldn't I have one too?

Don't know. Can your system even handle that?

It's my business if I shit myself, right?

That's a regular thing at your age, ain't it?

There's not a single thing regular at my age.

Tragic.

Nah. Keeps things exciting.

Thanks for spoiling it.

Just trying to give you something to look forward to as you approach my years, Cousin.

Yeah, the suspense was killing me. The medicine?

In my coat. I'll grab them, but you got to tell this twitchy little bastard over here to stand the fuck down. He ain't going to hit shit with that chicken wing, except maybe his buddy behind me. At that, I hear footfalls behind me move to my right, and I chuckle while the overwatch lowers his elbow a little, but not completely. I call out to him, seeing I've shaken his confidence, Hey, you, what dipshit taught you that, my cousin? Fucking Air Force. Fucked up footing, too. Weaving back and forth. The end of your barrel is looking like a metronome.

What's that?

Go look it up, I'll wait.

Fuck off.

Lean forward on that front knee while you're at it, turn that back foot out a little, and tuck those elbows into your ribs—get rid of that chicken wing. See, it's a fighting stance same as any other—boxer or trigger puller. But you're yet to pull a trigger on a man. Ain't that right? I can close this distance before you can get your safety off and squeeze off a round. That's if your magazine is even seated properly.

His eyes examine me, wonders whether I'm bullshitting, and does as I've told him.

That means to lower your weapon, dumbshit, and go work the gardens. Go!

These kids are still learning, Jon. And they know full well who you are. Anyone strolling up here like they're on some rooftop greenway is a little unfuckingsettling these days.

These Minutemen aren't going to cut it. There needs to be dedicated soldiers out here.

The dogs don't even fuck with you, for fuck's sake. Don't let yourself get so worked up. This the first time you've had a gun in your face or something?

Not if memory serves. Good thing this place is swarming with packs of dogs, huh? Got someone to do your light work for you, I see.

Thank God for small favors.

God? Fuck em.

Give me a hug, you prick. And what do you mean *fuck God*? You know it's your cousin who keeps dropping deer from the rooftop to feed these dogs, keep em close. There's no better motion detector out there.

Well, no shit.

Am I going to have to make you turn over your knives while you're here?

Make? Your boy with the wand didn't find a blade, I say looking over my shoulder to flash a smile to the guy with the wand.

I'm not stupid.

Do you want to search me? A little caressment would be nice.

Shut up, for fuck's sake. You weird out these guys as is.

Oh, I thought they were of a more tolerant generation.

Still, they don't know you. They just know *of* you.

That's not enough these days?

Sorry.

Well, what are you going to do?

Resist.

That was rhetorical.

Thanks, Professor.

Speaking of, how're classes coming? Is anyone going?

Handful.

Everyone needs to be up there at least a couple of times each week. You still got a copy of the cookbook up there?

Yep, along with every field manual we could scrape together as they came in.

From what I could tell on my way in, there's more than enough bodies covering the watch for them to be more than fighters. Rotate them out. Get them into the textbooks. It's necessary, you understand. We need thinking men and women.

They're followers. They were PFCs and Lances. Never taught to lead. Never taught to look at the big picture.

Don't matter. Fix it. They need to understand how this all used to be, I say pointing to everything and nothing. A coup will not work if there's no one to sit in the throne once we empty the damn thing. We need to fill every chair in the Duluth district council room once this kicks off. You do understand what we're working toward here, right?

They're not going to listen to that from me. If you want to see it happen you know what has to happen, don'tcha?

And just what might that be?

You have to come back. And stay, Shaddox. This place still has room for you, you should know that.

Yeah, but nothing should hinge on any one person.

Are you saying we're fucking this all up, Shaddox? Too many Indians, not enough chiefs?

No such thing. And if you say that dumb shit again, we'll find out together real quick like where my blades are stashed.

You know, I remember reading somewhere people mellow in their old age.

That's called going lame. You see any nursing homes around here?

Nope.

That's right. There's no time to get old. There's no pasture to be put out in.

Thanks for the heads up.

You ain't but, what, ten years behind me?

Giver take.

Give or take, huh? You stop keeping a calendar then?

Don't see the point, really.

Well you're entitled to make dumbass decisions as long as they don't affect the whole, I guess. That aside, can you tell me how many docs have made it here now?

Shit, most of them from the cheesehead unit. Along with a number of the docs deemed nonessential when the district's hospitals were collapsed into the one.

Good. Good.

Why? You want me to ask if any of them specialize in geriatric medicine?

Fuck off. I can see the Benedictines when the time comes. Let me know what they need.

What they need?

Yeah.

You the tooth fairy now?

Would you like to make an offering? I ask, smiling as I twist my fingers into a fist so loudly it stops the chattering of the two watching us from above.

No, they don't need anything more than a way into the satellites' supply hub. Can you help with that?

I'm not the one sitting on a surplus of former thieving lower enlisted and crypto-warriors, now am I? I'd say that crown lies on your head.

FLU-LIKE SYMPTOMS

Babe, how many sick days have you taken so far this year?

All of them.

You get how many a year, though?

That's not the issue, Jonathan. They accumulate. I've taken all of my cumulative days. That's on top of the days when I've come in late, left early for not feeling well enough to work. They don't even look at those days.

Lucky you. They know every time when my truck stops moving for longer than a red light. It gets recorded, somewhere.

So so lucky. Now they want me to report to work regardless of how I say I'm feeling, even if I'm on an approved sick day.

Okay, so what are they bitching about if it's approved? You've earned those days. You have the right to take them. It's not like you're taking vacation days and neglecting your patients while nursing a hangover or some shit. They know you're sick, they're seeing you as a patient.

Not anymore, they're not. Aside from the fact that they've deemed I only have flu-like symptoms—nothing diagnosable or curable, nothing that'll deem me nonessential—we have a cap on how many visits we are allowed at the hospital, even as employees. More so as employees. We're allowed fewer visits from what I understand. And I've exceeded that number already for the year. You'd know that if you ever took ill.

What if they fire you. You can get seen more often as a private citizen, right? Won't that wipe your slate clean for the year? You've got to get to feeling better.

Fire me? They just might, she laughs a laugh free of joy. They've already given all of my therapy patients to the others in my office. I'm only taking care of walk-ins now. But they won't restart my number of allowed visits over again if they fire me. That's not how this works.

Use mine then. I should have plenty. They don't start deducting until after, what, a decade, right? I've never even taken a day for the sniffles.

Never? Are you trying to say you don't recall taking that long weekend along with me?

Yeah, I do. You know I do. I remember every time that long weekend comes over with her husband and kids. That was a hell of a long time ago, though. There's no telling how many days I'm sitting on right now.

How do you not know how many days you have in the hopper? Do you know for sure whether you can share them with me? That would help everything, my God.

I'll check it out.

Why haven't you looked into any of this already?

They keep me kind of busy during the day in case you haven't noticed. They don't schedule me lunch breaks or allotments of time to complete administrative stuff like you medical professionals, you know that. And I've never paid any attention to that part of my remittance statement. Why would I even keep track of the sick days I've earned?

Yeah, well, babe, mine says deficient in every column.

Every column? Can they even do that?

They can dock your remittance if you exceed the allotted amount of medical visits like I have. It's how they get a co-pay out of me. I've cost them more money than I've brought in for them now. So, they're subtracting the deficit out of my pay and meals owed.

Are you working for free then? They have to credit you allotted meals while you're part of their medical team at—

No, they don't. They don't have to do anything if they deem nonessential.

They have to give me credits as long as I'm doing what they require. They'll let me live here as long as I log onto my scanner each morning, and they'll send sustenance down that chute anytime you hit the *summon* button as long as I continue to put more miles on the odometer of that vehicle of theirs. That they'll do. I'll work more and feed us both. And—and I'll tell the kids to keep away with the grandbabies, those little germ factories. Every time they visit you get sick with something else and have to go for more testing and end up taking more time away from your patients.

You'll do no such thing, jerk, I love those little germ factories. You love them, too.

Yeah, maybe. But if they touch my bookshelves again, they're banished.

Try it. I'll banish you.

You'll have to get out of this bed in order to do that. So, please, banish away, babe. Banish away.

Come here, lie next to me a while.

Eww, no, what, are you trying to get me sick?

Shut up and get over here.

Yes, ma'am.

Don't you ma'am me.

Hush. You're a grandma and a doctor. I'll ma'am you all damn day.

PHARMACEUTICAL GIANT TEAMS UP WITH AT-HOME–ANCESTRY DNA TESTING COMPANY

By Weldon Musana
October 17, 2042

COLUMBUS — Test results from over 25 million customers of At-Home-Ancestry are now being used by pharmaceutical giant WaltonJohnsonProctor&Gamble to develop new vaccines and medical treatments, the two companies announced in a joint press release Sunday.

This marks the largest partnership forged with the intent to leverage the blood quantum home-testing market, utilized to expedite census taking as well as ballot casting. To date, At-Home-Ancestry kits are the only in the market to be considered certifiable for national governance purposes.

"With us working together with WJP&G, we will catapult the development of medical and medicinal breakthroughs," At-Home-Ancestry CEO Tamara Nagel said during a recent press conference.

"Future potential At-Home-Ancestry customers will be prompted to participate in this scientific research when ordering their kits during our convenient checkout process." Nagel continued, saying, "Our new joint transparency agreement moves this consent firmly into the field of drug discovery and demand rather than its previous intent of merely quelling curiosities."

"If any of our previous customers do not wish for their DNA to be used in the forthcoming research and development, they can choose to opt out by responding to an electronic memorandum which will be sent out to their dwelling assignments sometime in the coming week," the companies announced in their joint press release. The DNA of those who have already transitioned becomes the permanent property of At-Home-Ancestry according to their current user agreement and can be utilized in any and all of the coming research and pharmaceutical development projects.

WJP&G has agreed to invest $2.2 billion in At-Home-Ancestry over the expanse of the six-year deal. This investment gives them exclusive rights to the DNA testing results needed to develop drugs and medically relevant care facilities curated for individual districts demographic needs.

Anwar Anthea, director of the Center for Pharmaceutical Research for the Public Citizen, said the only way for the two companies to stay within ethical boundaries is to make their service free for the customers who choose to allow their DNA to be utilized in said research.

"It wouldn't be unrealistic for their

customers to want to be compensated for the capital gains the two companies experience because of this endeavor and demand a sort of royalty payment either," Anthea added.

"Are they offering refunds to those 25 million customers whose DNA has already been analyzed and cataloged into their system so that they haven't paid for the privilege of At-Home-Ancestry to work with another for-profit company in a capital investment endeavor?" he asked.

"The NBC (National Bureau of Census) can ask people to report their genome sequences for blood quantum cataloging, but what is happening here is something else entirely," Anthea said. "It's upside-down when for-profit companies set out to farm DNA findings and expect customers to actually pay in to participate. It is simply not how scientific discovery works. Information like this comes at a price — and the price is not to be shouldered by the subject being studied."

Anthea went on to question the existence of protocols protecting At-Home-Ancestry customers born with certain predispositions — as well as those with pre-existing conditions — from being deemed a potential nonessential citizen.

This joining of forces has been years in the making according to the two companies' heads of research and development: Taylor Chalfant of WJP&G and At-Home-Ancestry's Preston Nelms, who began their careers together at another drug company, Tyrell Genetics Corporation.

"When a genetically validated target is dually pursued, it's twice as likely to become a medical treatment," Chalfant said in an interview last Sunday.

"This is for the good of everyone. The 25 million customers that At-Home-Ancestry has gained access to is ... I dare say 10 times larger, than some of the other databases out there," he added. "We both feel a responsibility to pursue this."

The biggest obstacle is to convince enough nonessential citizens to submit their saliva and DNA, and to pay someone to sequence it. At-Home-Ancestry's database catalogs an impressive amount of citizens who have already been deemed essential who, of course, are largely without the need of pharmaceuticals and medical treatments outside of preventative health.

Once the mass electronic memorandum has been submitted and responses are returned, the companies can conduct more sequencing on the DNA strands of people who have genetic variations of other interests.

"We are excited to leverage the nonessentials and have them be part of the discovery process," Chalfant said.

At-Home-Ancestry has completed some preliminary pharmaceutical development on their own over the last decade and has now announced they are excited to share their preliminary findings with WaltonJohnsonProctor&Gamble under the data sharing agreement and take the first steps toward production and distribution.

A SHADOWY
PROFESSION

You know, none of this should come as any sort of surprise. Poets and playwrights alike warned us, and warned us—warned the people, said something like, *Give them bread and circuses and they will not revolt.*

They got away with saying that? Kind of a juvenile thing to say, isn't it? No one shut them down?

No, not when it was billed as satire. You can say whatever you want with a puppet on your hand. The people will sit back and laugh and watch and wait for the intermission once their ass cheeks start to hurt from keeping their position too long.

How like life? Is that what you're digging at with this little analogy?

In a way, yes. Eighteen or nineteen-hundred years later, that turned into, *The people will not revolt. They will not look up from their screens long enough to notice what's happening.*

They waited for that intermission, patiently, didn't they?

They're still waiting.

What's that?

Some citizens are still waiting. Others are still snacking on bread while laughing at the clowns in the circus.

Funny.

Not whatsoever.

Why not?

The problem is that the people think they're laughing at the clowns, or with the clowns while they're making their own special brand of merriment. Most are yet to realize it's the clowns who are laughing at them.

Is that so?

'Tis. It has to be. Nothing else clicks in the brain. Men of my generation understood more about games than they did government. The people were polarized over allegiances, rivalries and such. They became beside themselves when their favored gladiators were traded. Some threatened a boycott.

A revolt against the games and circuses?

It was always short-lived. People relied on the games to escape and distract themselves from the daily. But there'd be burning of effigies, riots in response to hard-won victories. Police would patrol the streets with water trucks to keep them contained, put out the businesses and vehicles they set aflame.

They must have filled the prisons.

No, the revelers would be back to work and back to their daily lives right after they pissed the last of the spirits out of their system. Most of them still smelling of smoke. Their acting out was allowed. Justified as a necessary purge of emotion, an assertion ratified by district authorities.

You could pan for cobalt with the holes in reasoning like that.

Indeed, you could. Though the organizers of the games found a way to further polarize their audience.

How so?

By politicizing the games. Making them a patriotic show of allegiance or lack thereof, rather than one of brute force, strategy, bravado, and mindless distraction.

Sounds like the Senate floor.

Very much so. But they succeeded in making the pre-game sidelines as much of a battlefield as the fifty-yard line, making a mockery of military customs and courtesies.

And people boycotted the games because of this? Turned off their television set?

No, people would rather bitch than be bored. Some aren't happy unless they have something to complain about. Of course, they'd never dare say what was really on their mind. And, hell, most others had long since deadened those particular synapses by the time the spark of realization of what was really happening around them began to bother others brave enough to speak a word.

And you're meaning to say you somehow navigated your whole life while managing to stay above all this hysteria. How exactly?

Oh, not by choice. I wanted to play in the circuses since I was a child. But my grandparents didn't have the money for that. Not on my grandfather's pension. He was a veteran, too. Though, he never fired a shot. The war was something of a spectator sport for him. He chauffeured a general around a remote island far from the front lines, yet close enough to keep in radio contact. He eavesdropped on two years' worth of conversations while he drove to and fro. He earned no medals to speak of but perspective enough to last a lifetime. He shared his realizations and cynicisms with me, young as I was.

I see. How fortunate for you.

Not very.

I still went to war—on three different continents.

He didn't deter you.

He died before I could swear my oath.

I see.

Hunger and homelessness are huge allurements for we have-nots.

You don't exactly exude the aura of the proverbial door kicker or trigger puller.

After hygiene and first aid, camouflage is one of the most important lessons taught to new troopers.

That may be, but those manuals they teach you from are written at an eighth-grade reading level, are they not?

The advanced ones are.

And?

And what?

Sir?

Is this where you're wanting me to tell you not to call me *sir,* that I was a sergeant, that I worked for a living? Do you think what they taught me from those manuals would manage to feed me and my family once they were done with me? Or that I wasn't vengeful enough to take the money they offered for education and actually use it? They used me, so I used them. I stayed in college until I couldn't leave.

Couldn't leave?

Until I too became a professor myself.

He furls his brow.

I smile.

He relaxes his face some and the dominos start to fall in his head.

See*, they* offered to pay for education after you'd served them in order to lure in the dreamers, too, those who despised the life they lived before they donned the nation's cloth—the impoverished, raised by burned-out boomers. Later, as time progressed, and conflicts compiled, when theaters expanded until they overlapped becoming something of a Venn diagram with no discernable frontlines, when a soldier's life became a ceaseless nightmare, well, then *they* never needed to make good on said offer of education—for the most part. Most wouldn't venture toward another institution, ever. So the soldiers who survived the war let the offer of an education expire. And because of that outcome, *they* didn't have to make good on their promise.

Bait and switch.

A roll of the dice. Loaded dice.

And you did not become abject how?

I smile and watch his reflection in the windshield. He shakes his head, closes his eyes, turns away from my gaze. I tell him, See, from day one the sergeants stress you until you crack. They want to break you down, so they can build you back up in their image.

You didn't crack?

Oh, in retrospect, I think it's safe to say I showed up cracked and calcified. If I may, I'm certain that came about while I was still in my crib. The chaos *they* created was a circus, a show, a controlled environment. They could only do so much, and if they did too much, their actions were not without consequence.

So, they just toyed with you, basically?

With everyone.

And you toyed back?

That's when *they* put me in charge of the other privates.

From private to professor?

That's an oversimplification.

Excuse me?

An abridgment worthy of inscribing on a headstone.

You don't say? It's also for ease of conversation. Why are you behind a wheel instead of in front of a blackboard, or pacing a lecture hall?

You think I'm better suited for the Superior University?

You are a professor. Are you not?

They stopped educating educators.

Stopped educating educators? What do yo—

To start. A hundred and twenty years after they opened their doors, the Superior University did away with their teaching curriculum, failed to renew their accreditation, acted as though no one would notice they'd chose to abandon their foundations.

They were wrong?

That they were.

There was a backlash, you mean?

People simply went elsewhere or sought other vocations, ones which required more technical means of training.

No one objected?

Objected, no. People took it personally, the way they always do when something becomes out of reach.

Meaning?

Meaning they belittle it, devalued it. Acted like it was an abstract construct, one they didn't need in their lives. *College Boy* became a viable insult again.

Did you feel insulted?

Not from some proletarian name-calling, but when journalism was removed from the catalog of classes, I certainly did. More so when political science disappeared. Then history vanished from their offerings. That was the last straw for me.

You don't find that a bit melodramatic, even in retrospect?

Not remotely.

You're adamant then?

Absolutely.

But you didn't stick around and fight it?

It's not a battlefront. It was a business decision.

Capitalist principles applied to education, interesting.

Education too is a social program with a bit of philanthropy sprinkled about.

It is?

That didn't come off your lips sounding like a question.

No?

Oh, no. That it did not.

Journalism—or the lack thereof—*that's* what you found bothersome?

Unnerving would be a better word for it.

Journalism did not die when the doors to the classrooms got locked.

You're not wrong. However, ethical, introspective investigation did. As did the journalists who dared carry out such endeavors. Even subjective word choice died. People and the papers they worked for were told what to print, what to say, how to say it. The National Press Stylebook took on the look of a cliff notes guide. Those who once engaged and asked questions, quelled curiosities and caused discomfort in our district capitals, became deflated shadows of themselves.

Other universities followed suit?

All universities followed suit.

What bothered you about the disappearance of political science courses from the catalog? Is that what you taught?

No, but I certainly wanted the inner workings of our political system taught and understood to the coming generations.

Because?

So the following generations would recognize when something was broken, when something wasn't working as it should, how to fix it, and who should fix it, and how to go about fixing it.

The system worked once then?

We had something of an amalgamation—a perversion—of an Athenian democracy and the oral constitution of the Iroquois Confederacy.

A perversion?

When you adopt something someone else has theorized and put into practice because of the inherent good found in it and refer to those responsible for its establishment as *merciless Indian Savages* in the same stroke of your pen, then, in my mind, I'd say you've made yourself a perverter.

So, that would be why history has a special place in your heart, the good old days?

No such thing.

So why let yourself be bothered just because they decided to stop teaching history at the university if you find it all so bothersome?

History courses were stopped altogether, as well as the education of history teachers. That's where I take issue. Took issue.

Oh, you're over it then.

No. Not whatsoever. If history is not taught to the coming generations or if no one teaches educators how to convey history from a myriad of perspectives, to examine it under as many lenses as possible, then history cannot be learned from—progress cannot be made.

Oh, so we have a history of learning from history? Or had a history of doing so?

Collectively, we are a forgetful bunch. Individually though, that's where change is almost always spurred—or spawned—depending on how deep you dig.

Forgetful?

Be it from embarrassment or humiliation, any eyesore or a blemishment on an otherwise romanticized past, or the brutal reality of an ill-gotten, temporary foothold in a people's march toward the future. See, borders shift, regimes fall, but people need to know of the possibilities—that precedent, so history may repeat itself.

HELLO, WALLS

Welcome home.

Hello, Walls.

Shall I query a meal for you?

No, I ate.

Caloric intake?

Unknown.

Recorded. Shall I read you your notifications?

Clear all, please.

Deleted. Shall I list your newly received memorandums?

Route all to clutter files. You can play them some night when insomnia strikes.

Is this a directive, or sarcasm? Your voice is flat. Please advise.

Route them all to the clutter files.

Shall I set this setting as a default for future incoming messages?

Yes, for all but direct messages.

Settings updated, Johnathan.

Thank you, Walls.

Shall I initiate the shower with your settings?

Please.

Shall I delete settings for other users?

No.

I sense agitation in your voice, please advise.

You are correct. Leave those settings in the cloud, please.

Acknowledged. Setting a reminder to prompt you again in six months' time.

I don't consider that an acknowledgment.

It is my programming protocol.

Well, if you want to feel useful, I suppose. Be my guest.

The shower is now at your preferred temperature.

Thank you.

Music?

Please.

Preferred playlist?

Surprise me.

Very well, shuffling music from playlist of music originally released circa nineteen sixty-five to nineteen ninety-five.

You know me too well, Walls.

The path from the shower to the bed warms seconds before each step is taken in sync with the illumination of the walls and ceiling. The bed is readied, warmed to the body temp of a healthy human being, 98.6° Fahrenheit. I lie and say to the walls, *Slumberer number 2, please*, and the mattress top softens and molds to my shape and size, squeezes my side and shoulder and thigh to monitor my health while I sleep. *They* say it'll send a signal and unlock the door as well as light the way to my bedside if I fail to wake—die, expire, transition, in other words. I do not. Not this night, at least. Instead, I roll to my other side and stare at the vacant opposite side of the bed and deflated pillow. I'm not sure for how long I've stared when I finally come back to the here and now. This realization causes me to clear my throat and tell the walls to set the other side for Slumber number 1.

No Slumberer detected.

Slumberer number one, please.

Slumber number one is not detected.

Replicate, I say, and watch her pillow rise and then soften in the center while the mattress top billows and begins to take the shape of her sleeping on her side with her back to me—the way she would when we went to bed early enough to watch the sunset—one knee a little higher than the other. An arm appears and slides beneath the pillow and lifts it a little higher on its outside edge while her other arm emerges from atop the side of her hip. All at once, I see her neck appear then her bald head from which her waves and curls unfurl.

I too slide an arm beneath her pillow, move in a little closer. With my other hand, I take hold of the mold of her hand—the one waiting atop her hip—and, together, our hands travel down her side and rest on the mattress right next to her stomach in front of her belly button. I give her hand a squeeze, and the rest of her a one-armed hug. She's radiant, warmer than me. Warm enough to make me slide a leg out from beneath the sheets the way I did almost every night before she transitioned. *Died* is still too hard a thing to say. Her shape shifts closer towards me, presses into me, and I remind her I still love her.

She says nothing, the room is silent until the walls queue our recorded conversations, her part at least, so I fall asleep with her voice in my ears again.

POINT A TO POINT B

Could you at least tell me why you aren't bringing me along with you into these satellites? *They* sent me out here to learn all this, you know?

They did, did *they*? Is that what you think?

What do you think, *they* sent me out here to keep an old man company?

Old man? I mush my lips together and give it to him the best way I know how. He has to be the hundredth ride along I've done. You won't learn a thing, I tell him.

Oh?

No. You won't remember any of it, at least.

Oh, how do you figure?

You really think you're going to retain a single thing I've said to you? Your head is too spun up with all of this.

Hmm?

This being your first time outside of the circumcenter, and all.

Is that what you figure?

I do declare.

And how do you figure?

I wouldn't have said it otherwise. I'm not sitting here talking to myself, you know? I'm talking to you, with you, not at you. This is stuff you need to hear.

You're so sure?

I am. And I am not a fan of repeating myself.

How's that?

See.

What? Where am I looking?

See, you're not listening to half of what I say. Your heads on a swivel but you're forgetting to watch the road ahead of you. Besides, these women in these labs will be the ones to train you. They'll tell you what to do. All you'll have to do is walk into the lobby looking lost and they'll handle it from there. You'll be pointed in the right direction.

Well, that's something.

If you fumble around inside their lab, they'll get you right, or else.

Or else what exactly?

Or else you'll find yourself in a vocation elsewhere. Or. Else. *They* won't hesitate to send out someone new, understand? Believe you me. I couldn't possibly count the number of asses that've dusted off that seat for me.

I get it. This *is* day one, like you say.

I did say that, you did not hear me wrong. *They*

might send you out on your own somewhere tomorrow, too, you never know.

How many have sat in this seat? How many times have you had to train a runner?

You listen well. Look, all's you're learning from me is where to go, how best to get there. But I don't think you're even paying any attention to that. Well, I hope you're at least liking the scenery.

Sand dunes and crumbling concrete skeletons?

That kind of thing appeals to you? Does it please your eye?

It's new.

To you. I can tell you what to do, not how to do it. You'll have to figure that out for yourself. I do things one way, you'll figure out what works best for you. Or you won't.

I what?

You won't. You won't be in the vocation long enough to get a second chance.

I should write this down. Put it in a training manual.

Don't bother. There are no guidelines for this job. It's mostly unspoken. Get it done. However. No one will ask how you do so. As long as it's getting done, they don't care.

Scribbling this all down won't take much time or effort:

THIS PAGE INTENTIONALLY LEFT BLANK.

NATIONAL PROBE FOCUSES ON DESERT WAR VETERANS AS POSSIBLE EXTREMISTS

By Cynthia Dedmon
May 20, 2043

WASHINGTON — Earlier this month the National Bureau of Inquest launched an operation across the continent targeting suspected domestic terrorists including supremacists, militia, and so-called sovereign-citizen extremist groups. The probe boasts a large focus on veterans of the desert wars, according to memorandums sent from bureau headquarters to district offices.

The initiative was reported to be originally outlined during the final year of the former presidential administration, several months before a memorandum warning of intercepted intelligence of a potential insurgency — issued on April 8thby the Bureau of Internal Security.

The sentiments of this BIS report have sparked a rapidly growing ripple of concern among conservatives and veterans' advocacy groups alike. Internal Security Secretary Sabyl Embree held a press conference earlier today defending the assessment but stated she wished "to apologize to any veterans who saw it as an accusation or viewed any future investigations as their being unfairly targeted. Their inclusion is merely our being thorough."

"The report is merely an assessment highlighting possible points of concern which we feel our agents need to be ready for and wary of. It is not our wish to infringe upon the constitutional rights of the nation's warriors. This is not a group we wish to malign," the secretary said.

Documents outlining a surge in activity by domestic terror groups have circulated throughout the capitol since shortly after BRAC's most ambitious undertaking: the initial phase of the dismantling of the Armed Forces of both the former United States and Canada.

Numerous recently released reports state how the NBI's focus on veterans as potential domestic terrorists began during the final weeks of the Puryear administration when the bureau's domestic counterterrorism division foresaw the need to form a special counsel with the heads of the former Defense Department investigation divisions.

A redacted report dated February 23rd of this year, signed by NBI domestic counterterrorism leaders, released to the National Press, cited an increase in recruitment, threatening communications, and weapons procurement by supremacy, extremist, militia, sovereign-citizen and extremist groups.

The NBI stated their findings regarding the surge in recruitment are based on confidential and protected sources — which they will not give further comment on — including undercover operations, reporting from various district policing agencies, as well as via publicly available information such as virtual gathering platforms and extranets maintained by the different groups.

The report's focus is to get in front of the emerging threat and protect the citizens. The special counsel also seeks to address gaps in intelligence gathering efforts concerning these national groups and their remote cells spread out among the various North American districts.

The aim of the NBI's joint effort with the former heads of the Defense Department's investigation divisions is to "share information regarding veterans of the desert wars whose post-deployment mental health screenings indicated signs of disgruntlement," Secretary Embree said during today's earlier press conference.

Scott Doyle, NBI deputy director of domestic terrorism, said in an interview last month that the portion of the operation focusing on former military members related only to veterans who drew the attention of former Defense Department investigation division officials for their public criticism of the administrations they served under. "The original concern," he said, "was the potential violation of their nondisclosure agreements."

"This is not an inquest into veterans as a whole. We're not labeling former military members as a terrorist group," he said. "In order for a veteran to appear on our radar, we would have to find them using key terms or troubling phraseology to become concerned with them individually, or if someone they're associated with is established as a member of one of the groups we are surveilling."

Deputy Director Doyle said the NBI's special counsel reviewed the parameters of the inquest before it began "to guarantee any tripwires set do not violate any individual's civil liberties. However, once an individual becomes a person of interest, they will then be investigated through the lens of the Patriot Act."

Conservative lawmakers and talk-show hosts alike — along with several veterans' advocacy groups — voiced complaints this week after learning of an internal BIS assessment which asserted the inarguable potential for extremist groups to recruit returning combat veterans for membership. The Chairman of the House Homeland Security Council, Rep. Markus Emmerling, echoed their concerns.

This separate BIS assessment — leaked to the National Press this week after being sent to district policing agencies — cited the troubling willingness of military personnel to join extremist groups following the conflicts of the 1990s because they were disgruntled, disillusioned, and suffering from the psychological effects of war. These same issues are riddling today's returning veterans, as evident in the bloat seen in the Veterans Administration's Medical Care Centers across the continent. Veterans draw special consideration, the report said, because of their advanced training in guerrilla warfare and counterintelligence.

Rep. William Kregg of the Columbus district, the House Conservative leader, said he could not have been more offended upon learning that veterans are being categorized as potential domestic terrorists by the administration they once served and will issue an open letter urging President Geoff Burr to speak on this issue and sign an executive order to end the inquest.

Bobby Gordon, a BIS spokeswoman, said the report was issued prior to the resolution of an objection concerning a certain part of the report which was raised by the bureau's civil rights division. She called it an "embarrassing flaw with their internal legal processes" which should be fixed, though there are some within the organization who feel the matter is insignificant in comparison to matters of national security.

The NBI report shows the bureau has worked with investigators from the Army Criminal Investigative Division, the Air Force Office of Special Investigations, and the Naval Criminal Investigative Service, to identify those believed to fit the profile of a domestic terrorist for nearly half a century.

The report detailing the inquest is unclassified but meant for distribution within district policing agencies only.

HELLSCAPE

You're just now being let out of the towers, isn't that right?

Only...Just...As of late...However you want to put it, yes.

Allowed then.

Then? After all, I'd say.

After is not quite right.

Oh?

That's right. You've only seen the middle of this story.

Is that right?

That's right, and there's no way in hell for you to remember the beginning of all this.

I heard my family talk about how things used to be. I get it. I get—

Is that so? Oh, well, forgive me then.

You are forgiven.

Don't be so sarcastic. It is quite bad for your health.

What isn't these days?

Keep up the sarcasm and you'll get the great pleasure of tasting my dashboard. But I'll warn you now: it's not near as chewy as it looks.

Now who's the smartass?

You're mistaken. I'm an idealist turned realist.

Isn't that another way to say cynic? The desert sand does do that, from what I've heard.

That what you heard, is it? Call it a colloquialism.

He clams up, swallows a breath—holds it down in his chest—chews on those six syllables.

Yeah, now you're quiet. Smart choice. You don't know shit about what the desert sand does to someone. Stories are just stories. And no one will ever give you their whole story. You know, for every book written there's hundreds of pages, scenes penned that had to have taken place in order to give a character dimension and depth—pages no one ever gets to read.

There's some sort of lesson coming, isn't there? I've slapped the bear on the snout.

You—we live in grime, dust, filth. The shit blowing in the breeze around outside here ain't even enough to trigger a desert memory.

Well, in all seriousness, that makes me breathe a little easier. I'd prefer you to not flashback behind the wheel while going god knows how fast.

Well, optimism is good. But, that aside, do you really think there's an end to any of this? Do you?

No. There's no way, is there? No one wil—

No, there is not. You're just stuck in the middle of all this with no end in sight.

None?

Not that you have much to worry about. You were born into all this shit. It's normal for you, quotidian even. Those of us who remember life as it was before, we'll die off. The things we've managed to put on paper will be billed as fiction or alternate reportage. It'll all boil down the way it did for those from before who dreamt of unicorns and rainbows only to realize it was rather a rhino and the spectrum of light reflected and refracted when the shower of its piss soaked the ground it trounced. This, I say, pointing to everything and nothing, this is it now. This song is stuck on repeat.

In stasis, is that what you're getting at?

Purgatory.

That makes no sense. I sure don't see it that way. Not whatsoever. I've been in the circumcenter all my life.

Oh, I see. I get what you're saying.

You do?

No, fucknut. You think that makes you omniscient or some shit? Do you really think that? You've been led astray, I laugh and floor it through the intersection.

I've seen changes, failings, stagnancies, implementation of new policies, deaths of others.

You hear yourself? Sound like you're parroting

some politician. Plot twists, that's all that is, I counter and shake my head. Plot twists in the story you're stuck in. For every action, there is an equal and opposite reaction.

So goes the saying.

It's a scientific law.

Well, there you go.

Yeah, but see, people are social. Social science works a bit differently than laboratory science.

What, are you not so cynical to say we're all just a bunch of lab rats scurrying around the maze of the towers and the circumcenter?

Not quite yet.

What are you saying then?

When someone throws a punch in your direction—even if you manage to slip it—you're still going to get grazed, right? Reaction is never as fast as an initial act of aggression. Policy may replace policy like you mentioned, yes, but not before enough people—and the right, or wrong people—are painted in an unflattering light. Your years have been regulated by black and white policy. You've never known gray spaces.

Gray policies?

No, areas of polyphony within the policies. Ambiguities. Verbiage which smacked of foreshadowing—and not of the sort people would look forward to with joyful anticipation in their hearts.

So, did all that make you think it better to just

turn a blind eye to the changing in the world rather than sift through the slurry of stories?

No, instead I decided it wiser to turn my attention to the true policy makers.

The true policy makers? *They* are not those throned in the capital?

No, *they're* puppets is all they are.

So, what drew your attention then? Or whom? I should say.

The business pages of the National Tribune.

Of course.

Of-fucking-course, of course. How is that even a question?

Because I've never cast my ballot for a corporation, that's how.

Oh, you haven't, have you?

No, I haven't.

You so sure?

Yes, I'm positive.

Interesting. But I'm glad to know you're so strong in your convictions.

Well, you do know what they say about a man without convictions, don't you?

Indeed, I do. Do you know who fed us during the desert wars?

No.

McDonald's, Taco Bell, Burger King, Kentucky Fried Chicken, Baskin-fucking-Robbins, for fuck's sake. The company that ran the mess hall, the DFAC, the cafeteria—whatever you want to call it—was owned in part by the then vice-president. He made millions upon millions each month we were there.

Is that right? Seems odd.

Seems, huh? It was the same when we were at war with the Viet Cong.

Is that so?

Don't look at me like that. As soon as the president announced we'd be leaving, he caught a bullet to the brain while being driven through the district of Dallas. And the guy who killed him, guess what happened to him.

Everyone knows that story. He got shot too.

Yeah, he got shot, too. Someone killed him before he could say anything to anyone. Flashforward fifty years to when my commander-in-chief was asked when we'd abandon the desert wars and his response was that he'd leave that to his successor.

Smart move.

Indubitably.

Seems a thing or two was learned over in that jungle.

Indubitably.

What do you mean?

Look around, look around—tell me what you see.

Hellscape.

No, just a desertscape.

This desert came from the jungle, is that what you're trying to tell me?

That is indeed what I am saying.

Your logic is bulletproof.

No shit, Sherlock.

That makes you, what, Doctor Watson?

Whom. And Doctor Shaddox, if you want to be technical, smartas—

Okay, I'm listening.

Good. Good. I am so very grateful for such a captive audience.

A monologue is coming, huh?

More like a conversation to kill the residual hours of our day.

Okay.

Do you, by chance, remember hearing about back when *they* said we couldn't grow anything but pretty flowers? No more fruits or vegetables. Couldn't even grow an herb garden, for that matter?

Refresh my memory, if you would.

Once upon a time, homes boasted manicured lawns and perennial flower beds. The genesis of grumpy old grandfathers yelling from their front porches: You kids, get off my lawn!

Let me guess, you had an immaculately manicured lawn.

Nah, I mowed every Sunday, though. Religiously.

You mowed religiously on Sunday?

Yup. I built up most of my backyard with raised garden beds until there was barely anything to mow.

Seems like a lot of work.

Yeah? Seems kind of wasteful to water grass you can't eat, too. Though I blanched the leaves of every dandelion that sprung up on my lawn.

Whatever it is you just said, it's gibberish to me. You know that, right?

Dandelions are—were—a weed of sorts that people hated. But the bees loved them.

They loved them? Past tense? Were they of use then? The dandelions, I mean—back when bees were still around.

The dandelions were of use, yes. Atop that, the leaves could be made into a salad. That's the blanching I was telling you about. And before you ask, that's where you boil them for a few seconds and then cool them off with iced water. The dandelion blossoms could be made into wine. My grandmother had a good recipe for that. My wife, she turned the roots into tea. I'm sure there are more things that other people figured out to do with them.

They make something like that in the towers, the wine.

No, they don't. That's rotgut. Don't drink that shit. Don't *ever* drink that shit.

Rotgut? I can stomach it.

The people who drink that shit are the people who can't stomach this world.

I—have no clue what that means, and I do not want to learn.

You're welcome.

You're welcome?

You're welcome, I say once more, and nod. If you don't put that swill to your lips then I've done my job, haven't I? So, you're welcome.

Your garden, we were talking about your garden.

That's right. We were, weren't we? Where was I?

Dandelions, so many raised garden beds that you didn't have to mow, but mowing was your religion.

I deadpan. Religiously, it's something that's lost on you, I guess.

Oh, no, I get religion. It's still discussed every now and again. I just think it's an irony escaped by you.

Perhaps. Perhaps.

Well, I found it funny.

Well, yeah, I am here for your entertainment, after all. So it all works out all right. I'd plant my garden as soon as the snow stopped falling. Stores up over the hill sold soil, seed, and fertilizer. I'd grow everything I could in our short season: carrots, squash, beets, zucchini, cabbage, kale, mint. Mint would grow anywhere and everywhere. Their vines would spill out of the boxes along with the pumpkins. Tomatoes and cucumbers climbed the fence between my house and the next-door neighbors. Enough grew for me to give them the excess, when the weather was at its best—even with the bears treating my boxes like an all-you-can-eat buffet. Bastards.

Bears? It wasn't scavengers?

No. The scavengers are different. Homeless was what we called them then. I mean, we had scavengers as well. Or those who scavenged, at least. But they were scavenging for different reasons. They'd steal anything they could and try to pawn it off, so they could cloud their minds, scratch an itch. And you've got the wrong idea about the homeless, they'd never steal like that. They would not have to take something if they hadn't lost everything.

He deadpans.

The excess we canned. Tomatoes, raspberries, beets, cucumbers. You can pickle just about anything, really. Even fish.

Fish? How far into the fringes did you live?

Now you're going to tell me you've never ate pickled fish? You don't know what's good for you.

Ignorance is bliss. But, hey, I might try it next time I go fishing.

I deadpan.

I forget the year it was when someone decided vegetable gardens were something of an eyesore when stood up in the front yard, the same way a rusted out shitbox of a sedan was seen when it was put up on blocks to someday be repaired, someday. Nor did I care a whole hell of a lot when the district council came up with that little ordinance, being that mine were all kept in the backyard—as I said.

You didn't? You just watch from the front porch and sip away at your morning coffee, or something?

No, it wasn't like that. But, but it doesn't really matter what I didn't do now. I didn't say anything when the civil workers came out to my neighborhood to hand out citations.

I didn't say anything when they came back and ripped the gardens up by the root, either. Didn't affect me, whatsoever. I always had a healthy respect for rules, ever since childhood. I had that beat into me and knew if I just drew in the lines I'd be left alone to live my life.

Did they move their gardens to their backyards like they were told?

Well, no. That's the thing. It was too late in the season to start over.

That's unfortunate for them.

Especially, if it was meant to be something they stored until the depths of the wintertime.

That's really unfortunate for them then.

It's something the Duluth district council could have come up with before the spring season started. It was purposeful. *They* are not bumbling along, breaking eggs. *They* knew what it would mean for people would depend on that food. Don't kid yourself.

He mulls over my meaning.

Sometime during that same winter, some national legislator decided the potting soil sold at the stores up over the hill wasn't safe enough for the common citizen to use when growing produce. Especially the organic stuff. *Their* reasoning behind all of this was because it wasn't chemically treated against anything. It was just pure black soil, no deviation in color, no granules of perlite. The argument was made how there was no way of testing every square inch of the soil harvested and bagged and sold to the people. The worry *they* brought to the public was that it could come from the poisoned land purchased for cheap, blackened by a burst and abandoned oil pipeline. The people had to be protected. So everyone, nationwide, had to stop selling it.

So that was that.

Not entirely. I, along with many, many others, replanted the next spring. Seeds were still sold. Though, the nutrients in the soil aren't as plentiful when it ages, season after season, see? Therein lies the problem. The first domino to fall.

And the second?

Fewer things took root in the soil as the seasons went on, carrots, potatoes, pumpkins are mostly what still took root. You can only eat so much of that. And you sicken from the taste of mint. You can only put it on so many things, I smile a reminiscent smile while sucking some air in through my teeth, and say, The rest of that story is how my raised veggie boxes turned into sandboxes.

No, it ain't.

The soil dried out and my little gardens turned into boxes of dust and dirt is what I mean to say.

You mean like when the Hmong rake the dirt and call it prayer?

No, nothing that meaningful.

So, one day you had a bounty of food in your backyard and the next it was dried up and gone, dust in the wind?

That's pretty much it, yah.

No, it is not.

Isn't it?

Not at all.

Well, if you're so smart, why don't you tell me what happened.

I don't know what happened. But I do know everything didn't all fall apart just cause some senator made it illegal for stores to sell soil and then the next day there's a desert running smack dab from the Minnesota north shore all the way to the Rocky Mountains. That I know for damn sure.

To everything, there is a season. Lakes freeze, leaves fall, yada-yada-yah.

Do I look like a damn dentist?

Hmm? What? No.

Then do you want to tell me why am I over here having to pull teeth?

What do you want me to say? You want me to

say they crop dusted us with some sort of agent orange or napalm or whatever-the-fuck it was? We all thought fall came early that year.

To everything there is a season, isn't that what you just told me? You thought the seasons themselves changed out of the blue?

Stranger things've happened, you know? The leaves turned and fell. Lawns went brown and died. Even the pine trees, they turned orange and shed their needles. Then, around November that year, I guess, the storms that bring in the gales, they brought in massive amounts of heat lighting along with them, and once one bolt touched the ground the place lit up. Nothing new grew after that. Once the snow melted it was just dirt and dust and mud. Half the houses lit up like advent candles. Didn't your parents tell you about any of this?

They were afraid.

Afraid of what?

Saying something they're not supposed to, *them* hearing.

They don't care.

What's that?

You can say whatever you want. There's no need to censor yourself. There's never been one. Freedom of speech is something *they* thrive on. The more adamant, the more polarizing, the better. *They* want you to talk, and *they* want to hear. Talk all you want. Nothing bad'll come of it. I promise you that. Believe you me.

Just talk, blab away then?

Yes! Is that so hard to understand?

No.

Okay, trust me on this: talk, and the next time you walk by a billboard there'll be an ad displayed trying to sell you something you spoke of—new and improved and beyond your imagining.

That's not a coincidence? Not one of those things where you think about something and then all of a sudden you start noticing it all around you?

Shit no. No such animal. That never was a thing. *They* gave up on trying to surveil us, see. Hell, we got better at surveilling them. Drones could be bought any place. But, as life became more fevered, or moved at a more fevered pitch, I guess I should say—we gave *them* all the information *they* craved, everything *they* needed.

Why?

Why? Because people love to talk, that's why. And *they* love to listen. Lucky for *them*, our favorite subject to talk about is our own selves.

Luck?

It all happened once we were given outlets to pretend we had personal lives as well as private lives. They didn't come up with that, some little lonely college kid did while he sat holed up in his dormitory room.

You don't say, Professor.

Haven't I said enough?

Language is the lubrication of conversation.

THE TIME TO SHUT DOWN THE VETERANS AFFAIRS IS COME

By Karen Cazer

June 1, 2043

WASHINGTON — There is but one way to be removed from your vocation within the National Bureau of Veterans Affairs. Inflating patient numbers to entreat additional subsidies is not the path. Neither is dispensing either expired, obsolete, ineffective, or otherwise harmful combinations of pharmaceuticals. Practicing medicine in a manner which would guarantee a report of malpractice will barely solicit a verbal reprimand from the sitting Surgeon General. Indeed, the only way to be removed from your vocation is to blow the proverbial whistle on anyone who does knowingly undertake any of these aforementioned shameful matters. Or so says the National Office of the Inspector General who reported their findings to President Geoff Burr just this week. The NOIG is the agency to which government whistleblowers report wrongdoing, which falls under the umbrella of the National Bureau of Inquest.

"We're concerned with patterns where whistleblowers who disclose wrongdoings are faced with trumped-up reasons for termination from their vocations, yet those who put the most vulnerable veterans' at risk remain," the NOIGspokesman Stephen Ulmschneider told the National Public Press shortly after briefing the president. "It goes without saying that this should not be happening," he continued. "The sentiment is echoed by every citizen, whether they served or no, except, obviously, by the Director of the National Bureau of Veterans Affairs. That said, I proposed the president initiate reforms to be implemented within the VA's infrastructure as well as protections for whistleblowers."

President Burr, however, deems the only real solution is to get rid of the National Bureau of Veterans Affairs altogether. "The governance of the former United States felt an obligation to do right by veterans, yes. It has no such obligation to care for those who continue to incite insurgencies and undermine our district policing policies across the North American Territories. We have done nothing to radicalize them. No other demographic takes to violence if their medical treatment is other than satisfactory. It was a privilege for them to wear the nation's cloth in the desert wars. We can only suppose they entered into service with the mind to one day use our training and tactics against us. Who will protect us from them?" the president asked of his listeners in his midday address.

Voters need believe the officials they elect will be held responsible for the inactions the governance. Yet there is no oversight committee to blame for the endless stream of disgruntled veterans reportedly taking revenge upon the national governance since the time the dismantling of the nation's Armed Forces began. Who should shoulder the blame? Is there some solution which would quiet the violence? How many quantified citizens would put reforming the National Bureau of Veterans Affairs at the top of their list of priorities come the time to cast their ballots?

Is there a member of Congress or a senator who could be removed from the ballot because of the actions of a few disgruntled veterans?

Every representative and senator has raced to the broadcast news cameras in an attempt to voice their displeasure, but none are willing to accept an iota of blame for the VA's shortcomings and risk themselves becoming a future target of said insurgencies. But, despite their public outcries, it is they are who are collectively responsible for the disgruntlement and ensuing insurgencies. "Had they not ceded authority to the medical monopolies themselves, the nation would not know this state of unrest," President Geoff Burr concluded.

Burr's administration relinquished most governmental authority down to the district level as he entered his third term because he realized our nation is too large to be run from the center. When the national governance turned operational authority of the VA medical care outlets over to the districts where they sat, it seemed the districts were capable of the task.

Rather than falling under the budgetary restrictions of a national agency — or being subject to any forthcoming implementations of the Antideficiency Act — Congress decided upon cutting checks to districts at the beginning of each fiscal year. In addition to alleviating budgetary woes, veterans have district level elected officials who can be held directly accountable by voters.

As a result, veterans saw a curtailing of bureaucratic issues and a new focus on medical practice rather than waiting for treatments to be authorized by someone sifting through a slush pile of claims and applications of what should otherwise be an automatic entitlement.

Some districts found more efficient means of handling operations while others became overwhelmed and ultimately failed. Others were simply different — a deterrent to older veterans with tragically deteriorating health. The reasons for this are quite simple. The populace of veterans found in Phoenix is simply different than that of Columbus, so they will approach things differently — all the while there was a common records system stood up for data and procedure reporting that all district-controlled VA medical care outlets could draw from and report to, allowing all to benefit from the growing pains and ergo, lessons learned.

Now, under the executive order President Burr has penned, the National Bureau of Veterans Affairs hospitals will be shuttered, and veterans will be free to seek medical care elsewhere. The medical facility who treats them will then send a statement of expenses to the National Bureau of Inquest. If the veteran is not one who is suspected of being actively involved in or linked in some manner to the actions of an insurgency, the expenses will be paid in full. If, however, the opposite is believed to be the case, then the veteran will be held responsible for the cost of care. The payment, of course, hinges on whether the care provided falls under the category of essential care.

The National Bureau of Inquest would not comment on the exact number of veterans suspected of being involved in insurgencies, but the current number of veterans who served and survived the desert wars is approximately five million citizens — ranging in age of fifty-eight to twenty-eight.

SMOKE ON THE WATER

It was English, right?

What was English?

That's what you taught at the Superior University.

And what has led you to such an assumption?

What has led you to such an assumption, he mocks. C'mon, man, no one talks like that. Nobody.

You prefer truncated colloquialisms then?

I—I have no clue what it is you just said to me but I do know it was a question of some sort, so, I do know you are answering a question with a question. Maybe I was wrong after all. Maybe you taught political science and got fired when they dropped the subject.

No, no one was fired. We were merely given the title of professor emeritus.

Colloquialism?

Think of Crane's slum fiction.

What now?

Crude dialect, lavish profanity.

Neither he or I spoke after my comment. Not for a while, at least. We watched the road in front of us, waited for a dispatch to cause the scanner to crackle to life. Backing into the maintenance bay had long since become my favored place to sit and wait while the passing sun baked and cracked the clay that was once the expanse of the district's greenspaces—dedicated to both a Norse explorer and our sister cities sprinkled around the globe—which stretched atop the traffic tunnels moving from east to west, or west to east, depending upon where your vocation took you during your day.

You know, you swear like a sailor at times too.

I am a fucking sailor. Got it?

What were sailors doing in the desert wars?

Good question. That is a hell of a good question.

Is it one you are going to answer?

Yeah, well, some questions don't need or deserve answers. Others shouldn't be answered. Life needs a bit of mystery sometimes, understand? Answers flirt with the idea of a resolution and a resolution would mean you know everything there is to know about a thing when that is absolutely impossible to do so, get it? But, since you put it out there, the best I can figure is that when the Marine Corps became a second Army after the desert war became the desert wars—plural—it became evident there was a need for someone to carry out the expeditionary side of things.

So, sailors?

Dirt sailors, but, yeah. If you know your history, it makes good enough sense.

Oh yeah?

Yeah, sailors were once buccaneers, privateers, pirates.

What's the difference?

The spectrum of civility.

What did you do?

Whatever I was told.

That's vague.

Broad, really. We pulled people out of places they should never have gone. Secured harbors and airstrips for our people and allies alike. Went places to teach people how to deal with their own problems, pirates and such.

Pirates?

Yeah, pirates.

Pirates? Like, as in, yo-ho-ho, and a bottle of rum? Just how old are you? Pira—

Pirates have been around as long as people have been moving goods across the water. Make no mistake, there will continue to be until someone comes up with some other way of doing things. Unless, of course, if Burr keeps at it and isolationism becomes the way of the world.

Goods?

Anything that can be sold or bartered.

What about remittances?

We're fortunate to be able to work for credit. Others aren't so fortunate.

You think we're fortunate? Are you an optimist? I would have never pegged you as such. No way. No how. Not you.

I don't think, I know. I've seen. I know there are places around the globe more fucked than we.

You really think so? Even now?

Absolutely. It's not like little boys sit around and pretend to be pirates like their fathers before them. The pirates our governance sicced us after, their fathers were fishermen, as were their fathers. And, while we're on that subject, it was our corporations who overfished their waters and left them without a way to feed their families. A fishing village with no fish to eat or sell is sure to shrivel and die.

Makes sense.

So they took to the waters and did what desperate men do.

And it was your job to stop them?

We were just doing our job. We were good at our job. Lead'll stop a motor and splinter wood quite well, and the tracers we used lit the wooden hulls up faster than those men could bail overboard most of the time. Atop that, those malnutritioned men, high on khat, they don't swim so well, get my meaning?

No?

No, not while screaming for help. You need a little air in your lungs for buoyancy. A little fat on you will make things easier, too.

Help?

Yeah, well, we had rules, you know? Once one can no longer be deemed a threat, we were obliged to signal for someone to launch a recovery effort. But we couldn't do it ourselves; we weren't set up for all that. See, they'd been plunged into the waters where their grandfathers fished for shark.

Shit.

Some were placid.

What do you mean by placid?

Khat makes you high. Euphoric.

Where'd they get the khat if they were in so sorry a situation?

Their employers. Just like when the Yucatanians were under the employ of the Spaniards.

Servitude, you mean?

Sounds like you do read a little more than you admit.

I do.

Good for you. So you should know about how the Yucatanians were given coca leaves to chew while they worked, just like the pirates got khat. Probably still do. Some of those Yucatanians starved to death, fell right over, dead before their face slapped the soil they cultivated. Both khat and coca suppress the appetite and set people on autopilot. They don't have a care in the world, you know?

Zombies?

I suppose.

Hey, you've got to keep positive. Accept your fate and all.

Or rage against it. The whole works.

That sounds like a great way for a cog to get snapped off and spit out.

Only if it's one cog that quits. And I think the metaphor you're looking for is to be chewed up and swallowed, disappeared. But if they all were to, well, then the machine wouldn't work anymore, now would it? It would seize and cease.

What then?

What? Do you think cogs don't know how things operate? Those atop the tower haven't a clue. Trust in that.

So, why all this?

There was no proverbial straw weighing on the camel's back. Those who tell you that simply lack the foresight to notice the foreshadowing that was always within their periphery. No one thing is responsible for tipping the scales, not even Burr. Burr is a symptom of a parasitic system. He's not the problem.

What's the problem then?

It's a world of individuals. Individuals are easier to keep in line. And disappear. When we were grouped, unionized, galvanized, there was strength in voice. Now it seems there are only whispers, sadly.

So that's it then. Buckle up and wait for the ride to end?

I shake my head slowly and for longer then I imagine. Come to find out this is one of those times you think you've said something to yourself except you've said it aloud for all to here, but vice versa.

Are you going to tell me what you're over there shaking your head at?

You ever saw those green signs with the trinity of arrows twisted into a triangle?

Yeah. They're plastered everywhere. I see them all around where we dump the refuse.

Exactly. Let that marinate a while.

Meaning?

I mean they're a reminder for us proletarian types to reduce, reuse, recycle. Though, they're something of a hieroglyph. It's as if those atop the towers think those of us who live on the first few floors need to be reminded to think about what we need to throw out, what we need to hold on to, what we need to reuse or use in a more meaningful manner.

Well, if I didn't know any better than to take your words at face value, I'd almost say that sounds like something of a manifesto.

How do you even know that word?

Maybe you're just that good of a teacher.

Oh yeah?

Maybe I know it because you know it.

Maybe what now?

Maybe there'll be another desert war. Here.

You talk the way one does when they've never known war. If you'd ever so much as seen one—even on your television set—you wouldn't wish for one on your own soil. The last time there was a war around here was some two hundred years back. It's still a stain on the memory.

What do you mean?

Well, one side was, to put it mildly: outgunned. Then stripped of their—everything. Forced onto camps, starved. Then as a last fell swoop, they were exposed to a sort of germ warfare. But even that didn't work. So *they* went after the children.

Shit. That some kind of secret war? Ethnic cleansing?

No, the Indian Wars was what *they* called them.

How were these wars won?

Won? No war is ever won. By either side.

You have a point there.

It's a sentiment that's been echoed throughout history.

Is that what you taught? History? Is that how you know about these Indian Wars?

No school ever taught the history of the Indian Wars.

Then where'd you lea—

I extend my hand to shake his and introduce

myself: Boozhoo niij-anishinaabeg. Bangii eta go ninitaa-ojibwem. Ninga-kagwejitoon ji ojibwemoyaan. Jonathan Shaddox nindizhinikaaz zhaaganaashiimong. Baapagishkaa nindigooojibwemong. Gaawiin mashi ningikenimaasii nindoodem. Gete-ogichidaa anishinaabe. Mii o'o minik waa-ikidoyaannoongom. Miigwech bizindawiyeg.

He doesn't say a thing. He doesn't understand a word I said or even that I said a single comprehensible thing. And, really, neither do I. Not anymore. It feels like I'm parroting what elders taught me to say before anything else can be said. I tell him, When *they* waged that war, and we wouldn't die—when *they* came after the children—that's when *they* came after their tongues.

Tongues? It seems the tongues didn't die.

Not all, but some. Too many. Any was too many.

How?

When *they* realized the camps did not do what they'd hoped, they scattered us.

A thinning?

No, no. Sent us here and there. Forced or coerced integration, if you will. We found each other, though. Our numbers grew, and a reclamation began after two or three generations' time.

And then?

And then a resistance, followed by the decolonization.

De what? What does that mean exactly?

You know how the people have been resettled into the towers, fed the food we're fed, governed by this governancethat has been cast over us?

Not that I noticed.

That was *their* plan. The Indian Wars was their practice run. This, I say, pointing to everything and nothing, is the plan perfected.

And you're going to sit there gripping that steering wheel like it stole your last meal and tell me you actually think that some sort of a Second Civil War wouldn't rectify that?

Who knows? That's beside the point, wouldn't you say? You need to have soldiers to wage war, don't you?

Wasn't the first fought by farmers?

Yeah, but there's no more north or south to speak of, is there? Not since the Great Lakes drained down into the Great Plains and made the Great Divide. There's damn near nothing but mountains and marshlands on either side. Everything due west of here is dried up clear to the Badlands—beyond that, too, right up until you get to the Red Desert. Going south, or east even, you'd need a Navy just to kick shit off.

Boats we have.

Farmers we do not.

Say what now? I'm pretty sure every meal *they* distribute in the tower comes with a portion of vegetables and some sort of starch.

Right. It's seeded and fertilized and watered and sprayed and monitored and harvested all through automatonymous means.

You know that for a fact?

Can't you taste it? That–ah—aftertaste that clings to the inside of your mouth, even after you wash it all down with that water they pipe in from where-the-hell-ever.

Don't you think your taste buds have just changed a bit? Every seven years or so, right? How long's it been since your raised garden beds turned to sandboxes? Seven times what?

Point taken. I see where you're coming from with that, I do. I really do. But there are other things that are undeniably different.

Like what?

My piss after asparagus.

What about it?

It doesn't have the same tinge it once did.

Hmm?

Once upon a time, when you ate asparagus, your piss became tainted with sulfur. The warm wafting fog burned your eyes and nose hairs on its way up to the exhaust vent.

He wrinkles his nose, furls his brow, imagines it for himself, and lets me continue.

I tell you what, if you were ever in too big of a hurry to get away from the smell and didn't take a second to shake it off a time or two into the toilet bowl—you might as well toss out whatever it was you were wearing. Hop in the shower while you're at it. If any dribbled down your leg, that is. That was a smell that just would not go away.

Why the hell would you eat it then?

The wife liked to cook it. I did, too, but I could never get it to taste quite like hers. If memory serves me, she'd sprinkle it with oil and garlic, salt and pepper, top it with parmesan. Bacon sometimes, too. I liked the taste of it. Hell, now that I'm thinking about it, I *loved* the taste of it. I liked to give the dog some too before I'd walk him around the neighborhood to piss on everything his heart desired, make the other dogs think a damn werewolf had come on through.

MARY, MARY, QUITE CONTRARY

A fervent fist beats against the window with a knowing assurance that it'll never be enough to shatter said glass. Undeterred and despite the violence of action, the sound barely rises above the cadence of our conversation inside the cab of the vehicle.

Shaddox, just who the fuck are you out here talking to?

What?

One of the watches just told me you've been out here all damn day.

What?

Don't have me standing out here in the dark, man, you know I don't like those goddamn dogs. I ain't some Mowgli motherfucker like you.

What?

Open the damn door, Dances with Wolves.

What?

Now.

What seems to be the problem, Officer?

Shut it.

Shit. Calm down, I couldn't hear you. You know the armor on these is nearly soundproof.

Shaddox, tell me what the fuck you're doing sitting out here. I've got three shooters with you in their scopes wanting to put you out of your misery. They say you're out here looking like you've lost your absolute shit. What gives, man? These guys have got it in their head you're letting them know right where we are and what it is we're up to. Now, I heard you yammering away. So, I'll ask again, who are you in communication with?

I'm talking to this runner they've got me showing around to the district satellites, I say, as I shake my fist and point over to the passenger seat with my thumb.

He ducks down and takes a look. Jon, man, I don't know what the fuck you're talking about. I hate to be the one to tell you this, but there ain't a thing over there but your fucking reflection, he says and stuffs his pistol into his leg holster before he buries his nose and mouth into the bend of his elbow. Even with his face buried, I could see a sadness come over him, and his face fell. At that, I turned to the passenger seat and see that the runner's taken off and left me looking a fool.

Fuck. He bailed, I say.

Bailed, Jon? That seat's so damn dusty it hasn't

seen a set of asscheeks in years. C'mon, man. Come with me, I need you to talk to one of the docs.

I stare over at the passenger seat, look for a handprint in the dust on the door. But there is nothing of the sort to see. Something wrong with the serums I brought to you?

Nah, I mean, maybe. I don't know, man, they just said something about wanting to see you, okay? Come with me. Kill–kill the engine. Leave the keys on the mat, okay man. C'mon, let's go.

Okay, okay, shit.

For the first time in a long time, there's no search team gathering around to greet me. No air of suspicion. I'm free to enter. They know I'm a hunter, too. Always have been. It feels the way home should.

What's this?

Put it on, Shaddox. Put on the mask.

Hey, you can let go of my arm, I remember where the docs are. It's not that damn dark in here, you know?

Mask, Jon. Now. I got to escort you. You're a stranger in a strange land, understand?

Whatever you say. This is your house, not mine.

Shut up with that. We got this going together, you and me. But, it's just that things are a little different in here now. It's working, living, breathing, evolving. Isn't that what you said you wanted for all this?

Organic. I wanted it to become organic, bigger

than us, not need us. It's just me who's no longer needed though, huh? This is your baby now. I'm it's deadbeat dad.

It'll be fine. All right? You've taken care of us, guess it's time to pay you back now.

Yeah, okay.

Everyone, put on a mask. Do it. Don't ask, just do it. You, glove up and get that truck out of here. See if we can use it. It's going to need to be sterilized a good long while. Understand?

Sir.

Let the watch know what you're doing and to clear a path back from wherever you stash it. The dogs sound thick out there tonight.

Sir.

Let's go, Jon. Let's go see the docs.

They still down beneath the gym?

Nah, upstairs. Second floor. Remember where the principal's office used to be? Along with the counselors and the attendance secretary.

Yeah, of course, right across the hallway from the library. I spent enough time there, I ought to know. How many times did we get detention for fighting until they figured out we were cousins, I say, laughing all the while.

Yeah, we sure did. Didn't we?

That was forty-some-odd years ago. The shit we've seen.

Nope, Jonathan. Take the stairs instead. Don't want you on the elevator. Going to keep you out of confined common areas until the docs get a good look at you.

What now?

The elevator's out right now.

Oh. Okay. Stairs then.

That's right. We'll take the stairs then. How long have you been this way?

What?

Never mind. Just talking.

Oh.

Almost there, Jon.

Sending me to see the principal, I laugh.

Ha, yeah, man, sending you to see the principal. Sit down here.

I mock: Stand up. Put this on your face. Walk here. Stand there. Sit here. No one told me I was a damn marionette.

What's that?

I got no strings on me, I sing to myself.

Hey, doc. Got one you need to look at, quick like. Time is of the essence.

Yeah?

Oh, yeah.

Put him in the back room.

Got it.

Hey, Jon, got to move you again.

All right, Mangiafuoco.

What? Let me help you up.

I got it, I got it.

Okay, sure you do. Guess what?

Hmm?

You're going straight to the principal's office. Just like you said.

Oh, yeah. You're turning me in, huh? Do not pass go. Do not collect five hundred dollars. Go straight to jail.

Something like that. It's a treatment room now. It looks straight down onto West Fifth.

West Fifth? How bout that?

Yeah, just a few more steps.

I'm good. Don't get your bloomers all in a bunch.

Okay, smartass, I'm going to help you down, all you have to do is lean on back.

Too easy.

Close your eyes. Someone will be in to see you real soon. I'm going to close the door now.

Thanks, man. I didn't realize how tired I am.

I bet. I bet.

West Fifth—barely visible beneath the trees that line the roadway. Those trees tower above the houses they once kept cool with their shade in the summer. The houses that still stand, that is. My Grandfather's home stands second from the end. The opposite end. The blacktop that dead ends where the kids who lived too far to walk were let off the bus is still visible for the most part. Or would be, if the sun had not already set. So I close my eyes.

What's going on, sir? What did you bring me?

You need to quarantine that room. Quick. He's warm. Real warm. I found him in a fever dream talking to an imaginary friend.

A what now?

His reflection.

Fucking great. That's Sergeant Shaddox, ain't it?

In the flesh. For now. Haggard sonofabitch.

Heard about him. He brought all our stockpiles. I'll get some help, see what can be done to treat him.

Quarantine the room. I'm not asking.

Understood. Going to be a long night, I'm guessing.

I put a mask on him so he won't breathe on anybody.

Thanks. We got it from here.

Keep me updated.

Sir.

Hey, send two down to supply. We have to button up this back room. Have them grab some Tyvek suits too. Medium for me. Boots, gloves, hoods, respirator, goggles, you know.

Right away. You want me to call someone, or should I just run down myself?

Yeah, just run real quick, would you? Save some time. I'll steal a shield from the lab and go take a look at him.

All right, I'll make it quick.

Ah—is he gone?

Yeah.

Hold off on that. Get a couple of full-face shields to start. Elbow-length gloves. Let's not freak him the fuck out, you know what I mean? No telling what we got waiting on us or how fast we're going to have to act. Might just have to risk it. Is the scrub room ready to go?

Yeah, should be. Just put a new bottle of Hibiclens in there last week.

Is the decon shower set up?

The bladder on the roof is full, far as I know.

All right. You know where I'll be.

Have fun.

Not likely.

Jam some Bicillin into his buttocks and send him on his way.

He didn't come in on his own.

Oh. Oh—

Yeah. How do I look?

Like a walking nightmare.

Perfect. Perfect. These old guys are wound like piano wire.

Better you than me.

Well, let's see what's behind door number one, shall we?

Hey, try turning the handle first.

Fuck off. Get that shit I asked for.

I'm gone.

Hey—hey—hey, good morning.

Holy fuck. Why did I wake in the middle of the third act for—umm—ah—*E.T.*?

Still have a sense of humor, I see.

I see you have shit for bedside manner. Why am I here?

How're you feeling?

Oh, answering a question with a question. Here I thought you were a doctor, turns out you are a damn politician. Soon you'll be running the hospital.

You didn't answer my question, Mister Shaddox.

Well, you know who I am, apparently, so you know damn good and well I am immune to every goddamn thing there is, so that makes me doing pretty goddamn fucking good. Wouldn't you say, doc?

One-oh-eight.

Come again?

Your temperature is one hundred and eight degrees.

You need to check it again.

No, I don't. It's right. I assure you.

It's hotter than hell in here. I'm not running a fever. I thought the hospital always stayed nice and cool. Meat locker-like

It's sixty-six degrees in here. And you're not in the hospital.

Bullshit.

Your pulse is all over the place, and nowhere good. I'm going to take some tubes of blood, understand.

Ah—Yup.

What do you think you got going on with you?

I already told you. I am immune to every goddamn thing under the sun.

Is that so? What have you been exposed to recently?

What have I, I laugh. What have I been exposed to? Do you know what I do for them?

Please, enlighten me.

I'm a carrier.

Courier?

I transport medical donations for testing, to and from the satellites. Other nasty shit too.

I thought they called them *runners*. You're the one who brings us all our stuff.

You're welcome.

Mister Shaddox, do you know what we medical types call someone who is a carrier?

In this District? Mister Shaddox.

Well—it seems here it's one in the same, yes, but a carrier is a patient who is an asymptomatic carrier of a given pathogen. In other words: someone who contracts a disease through some means of exposure and then spreads it to others while exhibiting no signs or symptoms of the disease themselves. They thereby spread the disease to others, unawares. There's no suffering on their part. Unless, I suppose, if they were to end up inadvertently infecting a loved one with an infectious disease. Or a bouquet of them.

Are you trying to say I'm some sort of plague rat they allowed to wander around the city, all for the express purpose of thinning the herd?

No. I wouldn't say that.

What's going on out there, doc?

We're setting up a quarantine barrier outside the door.

Quarantine? But I have other boys and girls to visit tonight.

It's precautionary, Santa.

We'll run some tests, see what is going on with you. See what we can't do to get you out of here. In the meanwhile, toss everything you're wearing into the biohazard bag and put on a robe.

No.

No?

You'll give me scrubs.

That's agreeable.

None of those camo scrubs, either. I'm not going to be running around here looking like some kind of a dumbass in a stupid Halloween costume, you hear me?

Ocean blue then?

You are too kind. That'll bring out the yellow in my eyes, eh, doc?

I'm taking eight tubes of blood.

I take that back, you're kind of a dick.

I'll give you something to sleep, too. How's that sound?

Peachy. Just peachy keen. You sure you know what you're doing there? You look awfully eager with that needle. Try a ten to fifteen-degree angle, push it in until you see a red flash in the chamber, then you can start filling your tubes.

Thanks for the reminder. You are a gentleman and a scholar.

Well, you're half right there.

You have a good night, Mister Shaddox.

I close my eyes and he closes the door behind him.

I open my eyes to see myself attached to more tubes than I can count. There's a visitor sitting at the foot of the bed. The Runner. I'd say that alone tells me how everything they put me through the night before was a bunch of worrying and theatrics, but there is the matter of all these tubes sticking out of me. Or into me, technically.

Do you know the story of Typhoid Mary? Well, I suppose not. Misery may love company, but Irony is a motherfucker.

You don't say.

So, once upon a time there lived a woman the

world came to call Typhoid Mary. Posthumously, I presume.

Don't ruin the ending, I clamor, cutting him off as I lift a hand out in front of me, pantomiming for him to stop for a second and allow me to venture a guess, a gesture which reminds me again of all the intravenous tubes they've hooked to me. Typhoid killing her had something to do with the unfortunate moniker, am I right?

No siree, you are altogether mistaken. She died of old age, very old—for the time and place—and very alone for the last twenty-three years of her life. Or at least the last twenty-three years she was alive. You couldn't really say she lived much of a life. They exiled her on the isle of North Brother out in New York—right next to Rikers Island in the East River—as I understand it. She lived out her days in a hospital originally erected to house those stricken with smallpox. I believe you know a bit about that ailment's history, huh?

I don't have smallpox.

Neither did she, and that's not the point. But, since you brought it up, you don't know what all you have, do you?

I'm immune.

Think about it. They told you that you are immune, didn't they? Gave you this job. Got rid of everyone else. Made you think you were so exemplary that you worked everyone else out of a job. They said you'd be working as a carrier, which sounds like a courier, which makes one think it's just a matter of corporate verbiage—nothing worth dwelling on. Ever hear of the term Corporate Stooge? Want me to go find you a mirror so you can set your eyes upon one? They set you and the family up with a nice warm place to sleep at night in the towers—absolutely everything state of the art, not a want in the world. You got a key to the city. You can go anywhere and not worry about anything. You do have immunity, yes, but not the sort you think.

Kid, I say, and stop myself after it dons on me that I might be better off saving myself the time and energy, but not before telling him, You don't know what the fuck you're talking about. I'd hate to have him think I'd lost my train of thought or become distracted by some intrusive thought. Instead, I turn away from his nonsense and toward the window to watch the morning air move through the treetops.

He stands, blocks my view, and without moving his lips, says, Thou doth protest too much. I *am* your intrusive thought, and here's another for you: They knew what they had in you. You, a hardworking, disciplined soldier, who wanted nothing but a place in the world after not one, but two institutions turned out to be heartbreaking disappointments. You're like a shark who would die if he ever stopped moving, so they gave you a hall pass, and you kept swimming and you kept getting sicker and sicker, the host with the most. You slathered disease around the district for them, drumming up more and more customers for them, weeding out the weak ones for them, thinning the herd for them. They made you into a weaponized version of good old Typhoid Mary. But she only caused the deaths of about four dozen or so people, while you, you're a human smallpox blanket. How many do you figure you helped transition, outside of your entire family, that is? I'll leave you to that intrusive thought. Math was never our strongest suit.

NO STRINGS ON ME

A zipper unzips and Velcro rips and a door latch tumbles open and an asinine assertion rips me from the pages of a book where I've begun to gleefully drown in the ink staining its pages.

Your truck is rigged, I hear my cousin's voice say.

I say nothing. Instead, I blink. I wonder whether it was said as part of the conversation on the last page I read or if it left his lips just now.

Your truck is rigged.

Are you asking or telling me this? I say.

The dogs are gone.

Oh? Have you tried hanging a pork chop around your neck? I laugh. They might come back to play.

The vultures are gone, too.

Look out the window. They're circling. Way up there. You see them? Don't shake your head at me. Look. See?

Drones.

No, they don't soar or glide like an osprey does, but they don't drone about in the sky above.

They have sent drones.

Once more unto the breach, dear friends, aye?

C'mon. Get moving.

Come on? Get moving? Just how, and why? I've got these big, beautiful bay windows looking out onto it all. Yes, my friend, it turns out the revolution will be televised after all.

Get—moving—now.

How? I ask, You've locked me away, I say rising to a stand and plopping back down onto the bed just as quickly once my vision goes and turns the room into millions of shimmering snowflakes not white but gray ash not falling but floating but not that either hanging in the air covering everything around me not in a film or a sheen but hiding it away from me leaving me be in a blackened empty room with no more big beautiful bay windows to look out or a bed to lie on or a floor to stand on or walls to hold me in or a ceiling to keep me from climbing out. There is nothing. Then there is his voice. What the fuck are they pumping into you? They got you drugged up and we're about to die.

Hi-ho the merry-o / That's the only way to go / I want the world to know / Nothing ever worries me / There are no strings on me, I sing, and lift my arms overhead, until I feel my arms pinched and bitten from within and I take a look and I can see now and I see the bags connected to the tubes connected to me.

Shaddox, they are here.

You can't defend yourself against them. They will win. They will kill you one by one until there are no more if you try to defend yourself against them. They will tell your story for you if you try to defend yourself against them. If they decide to even give you column space.

Fuck. Fuck. Fuck. Fuck.

Life's a bitch and then you die.

What should I have them do then? Surrender?

Get me the cookbook from the library, please.

You hungry or some shit? Kitchen is closed, Shaddox.

The cookbook. Big, black cover, penned by a guy named William Powell. It should be with the rest of the field manuals.

You're going to do what with that?

Give them something to chew on.

You think I should call them back from their defensive positions?

Yup, I say, and add an unwavering nod.

What would you do, Jon?

You rage against the machine.

ATTEMPTED MILITARY COUP UNDERWAY IN DULUTH DISTRICT

Distributed by the National Press for Immediate Release

Monday, August 13, 2045

An attempted coup is underway by former members of the North American Armed Forces in the district of Duluth, according to officials. Preliminary details of the same are being reported in Atlanta, Olympia, Cleveland, Denver, Phoenix, Washington D.C., Columbus, Dallas, Chicago.

This is a developing story. Please check back for updates.

ACKNOWLEDGMENTS

This book results from sitting alone inside a delivery vehicle for eight hours a day for nearly two years on end (2016-2018). It was this that got me wondering about a dozen different "what-ifs." Unfortunately, more than a few of those fears have since come to fruition. *The Essentials* is a story of late capitalism and a populace comfortably numb with consumerism—even when profits get prioritized over people. "They" were the original antagonist in this story, but "We, the People" became the problem before an editor ever sank their teeth into this manuscript. Special thanks are owed to Miette Gillette and Michael Russell Jones for sifting through this book, seeing what I was reaching for, and wanting to share it with the world as much as me. Mostly, thank you to Jeremy, Kara, Monica, and Deb for looking at this book when it was just a skeleton. Hopefully, what is now between these pages casts a large enough shadow for folks to take note.

ABOUT THE AUTHOR

David Tromblay served in the U.S. Armed Forces for over a decade before attending the Institute of American Indian Arts for his MFA in Creative Writing. His essays and short stories have appeared in storySouth; Mystery Tribune; Michigan Quarterly Review; RED INK: International Journal of Indigenous Literature, Arts, & Humanities; Pank Magazine; The Dead Mule School of Southern Literature; Yellow Medicine Review; Open: Journal of Arts & Letters; Watershed Review; FIVE:2: ONE Magazine; BULL: Men's Magazine, and forthcoming in Red Earth Review.

Titles in 2021 include a memoir, AS YOU WERE, published by Dzanc Books, a novella, SANGRE ROAD, from Shotgun Honey Books, and this novel, THE ESSENTIALS: A MANIFESTO, which you've just read.

He currently lives in Oklahoma with his dogs, Bentley and Hank.

ABOUT THE PUBLISHER

Whisk(e)y Tit is committed to restoring degradation and degeneracy to the literary arts. We work with authors who are unwilling to sacrifice intellectual rigor, unrelenting playfulness, and visual beauty in our literary pursuits, often leading to texts that would otherwise be abandoned in today's largely homogenized literary landscape. In a world governed by idiocy, our commitment to these principles is an act of civil service and civil disobedience alike.

CPSIA information can be obtained
at www.ICGtesting.com
Printed in the USA
LVHW081649240121
677365LV00010B/737

9 781952 600067